FINDING JOY

ADRIANA HERRERA

ALSO BY ADRIANA HERRERA

American Dreamer

American Fairytale

American Love Story

American Sweethearts

Mangos and Mistletoe

He's Come Undone

Here To Stay (August 2020)

American Christmas (November 2020)

DON'T MISS MY NEXT RELEASE!

Sign up for my newsletter for updates.

OR VISIT ADRIANAHERRERAROMANCE.COM

Finding Joy
Written and published by Adriana Herrera
Cover Art by Leni Kauffman
Cover Design by Cate Ashewood
Edited by Mackenzie Walton
Copyright © by Adriana Herrera

To Addis Ababa, the New Flower, and Abyssinia—the homeland of my heart.
Betam amaseganallo.

"Wasn't that the definition of home?
    Not where you are from, but where you are wanted."
    — Abraham Verghese, Cutting for Stone

CHAPTER 1

Addis Ababa, Ethiopia
January

As soon as I stepped out of the airport, I felt it. The *something* in the air my mom always mentioned when she talked about Addis.

I looked around the crowd waiting for the recent arrivals as I hefted my huge backpack, searching for a big white head of hair. "À la Don King" my mother had said when she described Tefare, my parents' old driver from when they first lived here almost thirty years ago—who was picking me up tonight. I finally spotted a man with a mass of fluffy gray hair in the back, and walked over. I kept my eye on Tefare, who was scanning the crowd as he held up a sign that read *MR. WALKER.*

I stepped up to him, extending my hand "Tefare. It's me, Desta."

Immediately he threw his arms out and pulled me in for an elaborate hug. We bumped shoulders on either side and clapped each other's backs for what felt like minutes.

"Desta, you look just like your mama. How is my friend Fatima? Does she still make that delicious meat soup?"

I smiled at the mention of sancocho; my mother told me that Tefare had been a devoted fan of the Dominican stew whenever she made it in the old days.

I shook my head at his question as we walked together to the parking lot. "She doesn't make it that much anymore. She's vegan now. Only eats fasting food."

He gasped like I'd told him she'd given up eating altogether. "Only fasting food. No meat?"

I grinned at the shock in his voice. "No meat," I repeated as Tefare shook his head in silence, like the whole situation was too far gone to comment on.

When we got to the car, he made a big show of taking the backpack from me and putting it in the trunk. "Let me help you with this, Desta. It's too heavy for you."

I laughed because Tefare was not much taller than my five-foot-nine and had to be pushing seventy, but I let him win and handed him my massive backpack. Once we had my two bags securely in the back of the car, he pulled a hat out of his suit jacket pocket and perched it on his head. It was a 2004 Boston Red Sox World Series Championship hat, which looked exactly like the one my dad had been wearing the last time I saw him leaving for the airport on his way here.

I pointed at his head, smiling. "I recognize that."

Tefare clicked his tongue at my words, the happy, open expression from before replaced with genuine sorrow. "Your papa gave it to me on that last trip. I was waiting for him just like I waited for you tonight, and the first thing he did was take the hat off his head and put it on my mine. He said, 'Tefare, our guys finally won.'" Tefare's smile was a wistful thing, and I realized that my time in Ethiopia would probably be filled with moments like this.

"When your papa and mama first came here, there were only a couple of places where they could see the baseball games, and I would drive them there," my father's old friend explained, his eyes faraway, like he was recalling those times. "After a while he'd invite me to watch with them and taught me the rules. Paul made me a Red Sox fan for life."

Tefare and I stood there for a moment in the cold Addis night, lost in our memories of my father. Eventually he pushed off the side of the car where he'd been leaning and grunted, squeezing my shoulder. "I miss my friend."

I nodded, working on speaking through the knot in my throat. "We miss him too." It was hard to know what else to say. The moment felt too big for platitudes, and I'd learned years ago that when it came to grief, words usually didn't do much.

Tefare tapped the top of the car, then waved toward the passenger side. "Eshi, Desta, let's get you to the guest house."

I smiled when I heard him say *eshi*. It was like the equivalent of "okay" in Amharic and my dad would always tease me, saying it'd been my favorite word as a baby. "I'm ready. I'm tired of airports."

He stopped then and looked at me over the roof of the car, his expression mischievous. "Are you hungry?"

I braced for what I knew was coming.

"I don't know if I can find any injera and ketchup for you right now." He busted up laughing, and I smiled in return. My mom warned me to expect jokes from friends who knew us from when we lived here. Apparently, I'd been notorious for my obsession with what could only be described as an unusual combination of Ethiopian sour flatbread and ketchup.

I laughed at his delight. "I'm good. I like injera *without* ketchup these days. I ate on the plane, actually, so I'm fine."

I got in the car, listening to Tefare's low and friendly laughter. Once inside, I looked around the interior; the thing had to be at least twenty years old. But other than it looking like the inside of an old oilcan, it ran great. We navigated the streets of Addis, and I stared out the window at what had been my home for the first few years of my life. My feelings about this place had always been bittersweet. It was where my parents said they lived their happiest years, and it was also the place where my father died.

In three years of working for Aid USA, I'd travelled all over Africa, and somehow had managed to avoid an assignment to one of the biggest offices in the continent. I hadn't sought out coming here. But after my love life went up in flames, a last minute opportunity to help wrap up an impact evaluation seemed like the perfect excuse to get out of DC for a while. And to hopefully do some soul-searching about where I was going with my life.

Tefare looked over at me and smiled as thoughts swirled in my head. "So how does it feel to be in your first home? Are you happy to be back?"

I met his eyes in the rearview mirror as I came up with a response. I couldn't really say *yeah, it should be a good way to put some distance between me and my asshole ex.* I wasn't about to get into a long story about my Big Gay Drama with Tefare.

"It's good to be here," I said with a lot more certainty than I was feeling. "I've been nervous about the visit. I haven't been here since I was little, and after Dad died, I wasn't sure if I'd ever be able to come back."

No matter how much I'd prepared for it, this trip was a big deal, and a long time coming. I'd always found excuses to take other jobs when postings in Ethiopia came up, because deep down, I'd been scared of how being here would feel. Now that I was, there was a comfort and a familiarity I hadn't expected.

Tefare grunted as he turned onto a gravel street off the main road. "You had to come back here, Desta. Even if you left when you were only three, this was your first home. You took your first steps here, and your father loved this land. He died alone." The hitch in Tefare's breath was a reflection of my own reaction to his words. When he spoke again, he had that same bleak tone from before. "And that's a pain in my heart still, but he was in a place he cherished, and that cherished him back."

I sighed, looking out of the window as we bumped along the dark road, strangely comforted to know the people who had known him here still cared this much about my dad. "He did love it here."

Tefare nodded as he slowed the car in front of a tall metal gate. He flicked the high beams on and off and stepped on the gas to alert the night guard that someone was outside. After a few seconds, a man came out and opened the gate for us.

We drove in and parked right by a large yard. I looked over and saw there were flowers blooming on a crawling vine covering most of the fence that surrounded the property. The air was sweetened by their smell, and there was a light mist that kissed my skin as we made our way into the front of the building.

Tefare waved a hand around as he pressed the buzzer on the door. "This is a nice guesthouse, only embassy people. I came by earlier today and gave them some food and water bottles for your room. I will be back tomorrow morning to take you to your office."

Just as I was about to thank him, an attendant came to open the door and ushered me inside. I turned to shake Tefare's hand, but he pulled me in for a hug. "Eshi, Desta."

"Thank you for coming to get me so late. I appreciate it. I don't have to be in the office until noon, so you can come for me at eleven. That way we'll both get some sleep."

I watched Tefare slowly walk to the car, the scent of jasmine and the cold night air enveloping me. As I made my way inside I thought that in such a short time Addis already seemed to be getting under my skin.

* * *

"Wow, is this normal?" I asked Tefare as we drove past another security checkpoint in our attempt to get into the U.S. Embassy, where I'd be working. It wasn't exactly out of the ordinary to go through heavy security when visiting U.S. embassies around the world, but it was not easy to get used to either. This place was like a hybrid between a fortress and a very fancy suburb. The grounds were enormous. I was a little blown away as we drove through a small street lined with tall eucalyptus trees.

"This may be one of the biggest embassies I've been in," I said to Tefare as I swiveled my head, taking in all the houses and buildings.

"Yes, this is one of the oldest embassies in Addis, from the time of King Menelik, more than a hundred years old."

I nodded as he turned onto a smaller road. "I think I knew that," I mused, remembering my dad's stories about an Ethiopian monarch granting old allies like the U.S. and Britain acres of land for their embassies.

A while later we drove up to a set of buildings enclosed by rows of eucalyptus trees. "This is it, Desta." Tefare pointed.

After saying a quick goodbye, I exited the taxi and made my way toward the taller building with the sign that read *Aid USA*, hoping it was where I needed to go. As soon as I walked into the lobby, a lovely woman with an impressive mass of honey-colored curls and the most amazing cheekbones I'd ever seen showed me to my new boss's office.

From the moment I met her, I knew Bonnie Watts and I were going to hit it off. She was tall—a bit taller than me—with very curly white hair, which she kept on a messy bun on top of her head. Bonnie was wearing a flowy tunic over loose jeans and had gold Birkenstocks on her feet. The patented expat look, but she wore it well. She also had deep laugh lines and the most mischievous blue eyes.

"You must be Desta," she said as she stepped around her desk, her hand extended. "I'll be the person you complain to for the next eight weeks."

I laughed while shaking her hand, a weird flutter in my stomach. Anticipation, I supposed. All of this felt *big*.

Bonnie kept chatting around the friendly smile on her lips while I turned my head, taking the place in. "I can't guarantee anything you're supposed to accomplish here will actually get done, but I promise to take you out for beers when the shit hits the fan."

I laughed at that. "The most important part is covered then."

Her smile lifted into a full grin. "You got it. And seriously, thank you again for being willing to come on such a short notice. I know it was a big ask."

I could already tell she'd be a good boss. From my experience in this kind of work, a sense of humor went a long way.

"You're welcome. I'm glad to be here." To my surprise, I really meant it.

"Good man. I like you already." In a way, she reminded me of my dad. Bonnie had that same ever-present adventurous streak, with a glint of trouble brewing just under the surface.

"Desta, you'll be in the cubicle next to Sam's." She lifted a hand to a row of cubes right in front of her office. "You'll meet him tomorrow in Awassa." The eye-rolling when she mentioned Sam was interesting. "He's been there for a few days trying to meet some people and get some surveyors set up for you guys. He's a bit of shithead—"

Awesome.

"—and he will most likely piss someone important off before this is all said and done. But he can run data like a wizard, and we're hard up right now."

I did not like the sound of that, and I was sure Bonnie could tell. She waved a finger in my direction, as if trying to contain whatever was happening on my face. "Your job will be to run these surveys *and* to be kind to the local staff. Because they'll be busting their asses to get us the data we need, and you'll need to overcompensate for the fact that the guy running the numbers is an asshole."

I rolled my eyes and smiled at her directives. "You're pretty good at giving shitty orders in ways one can't say no to."

She laughed as I fretted about Sam's shithead ways. I could fake it 'til I made it with the best of them, but I had hard limits when it came to expats acting like assholes to the staff in the field offices.

"I'm sure I'll be able to handle him," I assured her. I'd been around enough to not put up with bullshit from overzealous dude-bros trying to show off. "So how will I get to Awassa?" I asked, trying to get the more practical details in order. "Will I get a car to drive down there, or will I have a driver?" I knew me driving would probably involve a visit to a local government office to sort out a driving permit, and wanted to get it cleared up if that were the case.

Bonnie flicked her hands like I was talking nonsense. "Oh no, you won't be driving yourself." She sounded like I'd suggested I was going to fly myself there. "You haven't been here! There's a learning curve,

7

my friend. You'll go down with Elias, the logistics coordinator for our project." Her face lit up at the mention of the man, which I guess was a good sign. "Eli's a star, one of my favorite people." Her grin got wider with every word spoken about the magical Elias. "He was a driver for a few years before getting the coordinator job. He'll get you there in one piece."

I could work with that. "Sounds good."

"He'll come by your guest house tomorrow at 6:00 a.m. to pick you up. Make sure you're ready to go by then—it's about five hours to Awassa, and I'd like you to be there by midday."

She waved a hand in the direction of the cubicle I was supposed to occupy. "All the stuff you need to go over is there. There's a copy of the contract, so you know exactly what we need to deliver on. The IT guys will come in an hour or so to set you up. They'll have a phone with a SIM card for you too."

She pushed off the desk she'd been leaning on and offered me another warm smile. I could not say I was feeling unwelcome in Addis Ababa. "I need to get to a meeting, but I'll be back before you leave. We're so happy you're here and can't wait to put you to work."

I laughed again as I dropped my backpack on the chair in my desk. "I'm glad to be here too."

As Bonnie walked away, I found that I meant every word. I could say it had to do with Tefare and Bonnie being the only two people I'd interacted with so far. But it was more than that. I felt at home here in a way that I rarely felt anywhere.

CHAPTER 2

I woke up to another chilly Addis morning, and quickly realized I had overslept.

My ride would be here to pick me up in less than fifteen minutes, and of course I'd be a whole-ass mess when he got here. I jumped out of bed and got myself packed up for my trip. Since I'd barely taken anything out of the bag to begin with, I was done in a couple of minutes. I did a quick wash-up in the bathroom and was stepping out onto the guesthouse parking lot with my shoes in my hands when a white SUV pulled up next to me. The top of the truck was piled high with what looked like footlockers, which probably held supplies for the field offices and some of the materials we would need to run our survey. I smiled to myself at the familiar sight, which promised weeks of adventure and hard work.

When the driver jumped out of the vehicle and came around to my side, I finally got a good look at him.

He was *not* what I was expecting. For some reason, I'd envisioned Elias as some sort of Tefare doppelgänger. And why my stupid mind decided all Ethiopian men were seventy years old with Don King hair would remain a question for the ages.

No, Elias was beautiful.

He was very tall. Had at least five to six inches on me, and his movements were easy and fluid as he approached.

"Hi Mr. Walker, my name is Elias Fikru." He smiled as he shook my hand, and all I could do was stare. "I'll be driving you today and for the time you're in the field."

His eyes were a deep brown, like dark roasted coffee, and his smile was warm and friendly. I needed to look away. One thing I was very aware of was that same-sex relationships were still very much illegal in Ethiopia. I had researched before coming, and as far I could tell there didn't appear to be outward violence like in other countries, but it certainly didn't mean it was okay to make eyes at guys I was working with.

Checking out a colleague within thirty seconds of meeting him definitely did not qualify as proceeding with caution.

A colleague who would apparently be driving me for the whole trip. And because my caffeine-deprived brain was a hell of a liability, I opened my mouth without thinking. "I thought you were the logistics coordinator. Why are you driving me the whole time?"

He laughed, and I felt the ripples of it in a place that had no business waking up for this. "I'm used to driving in the areas we'll be working in and I need to be there anyway, so I usually drive when the projects are in the south."

I nodded dumbly at his perfectly reasonable explanation, and stretched my hand out with as much professional demeanor as I could manage. For someone who had his shoes in his hand and probably epic bed head. "That makes sense. Nice to meet you, Mr. Fikru. Please call me Desta, and thanks for getting me so early."

He widened his eyes when he heard my name, which only twenty-four hours into my time in Ethiopia was beginning to feel like a compulsory reaction. My first name, Desta, means *joy* in Amharic, one of the official languages of Ethiopia. And my parents had given me "Joy" in English as a middle name to really hammer in that I would be a happy guy.

Once, when I asked him about my name, my dad told me when I was born, it was the only word he and my mom could think of. They'd been young and in love, with a new little person in their family, and were about to embark on another adventure, so I was double the joy.

My name had always been a source of infinite delight for any Ethiopian person I met, and it seemed like Elias would not be the exception.

"Very nice to meet you, Desta, and please call me Elias." His face transformed as he gave me a bright smile. "Your name is Joy," he said with genuine amazement in his voice.

I dipped my head, not sure how bubbly to be about this. "Yes, it is." His eyes on me were doing things, so I decided to veer from anything that prompted hard staring. "I was told to look out for camels."

He tipped his chin up in the direction of the road and lifted a hand, waving it back and forth. "Some pastoralist tribes do walk their animals around to find watering holes and pasture this time of year, so we may see camels on the road," he assured me with another wide grin. "It's quite a sight, long lines of them walking in perfect order."

I nodded as he talked, excited for the idea. "That will be cool to see," I said, tucking my shoes under my arm, ready to get on the road. That's when Elias finally looked down at my feet and laughed, a deep, rough sound like his voice was still waking up.

He pointed at the ground by my feet. "No time for shoes, huh? Or are you trying to be the American Abebe?" His eyebrows lifted, and I swooned a little. And seriously, what the hell? The man had perfect eyebrows, and why was I even noticing that?

Who gets hot for eyebrows?

Me, apparently.

I glanced up at him, feeling sheepish about my disheveled state. "Oh, I wouldn't presume to walk in Abebe's footsteps, with or without shoes." Abebe Bikila was a source of great pride for Ethiopians, who in 1960 won gold for long-distance running in the Rome Summer Olympics. He ran the entire twenty-six miles barefoot.

Elias made a sound of approval, like he appreciated my knowledge of one of Ethiopia's greats. "Desta, you're practically Habesha!"

I shook my head at him for saying I sounded like a native Ethiopian. I knew I had to be blushing. This gorgeous man's attention had me a little flustered. "I wouldn't quite hand me the Habesha card yet."

He laughed again, and holy shit was I going to have to watch myself with this man.

"I need to hear how you got your name some time. But first," he said, gesturing to the passenger side of the truck. "Did you have your breakfast yet, or some coffee? If you're in Ethiopia, you cannot start the day without getting some bunna. We can get you something before getting on the road."

His accent was also going to be an issue. His voice was so deep, and the lilt with which he spoke English was giving me shivers. There went those eyebrows again. It made him look rakish and I wanted to *climb him*. The lack of caffeine had to be partly responsible for the eyebrow fixation. I wasn't functioning at my full capacity.

"Sure, that would be great, actually." Wasn't I the eager beaver this morning? "I haven't eaten yet. I decided to forgo food and get more sleep," I confessed while I moved to open the passenger door. "I'm definitely still jet lagged too. And I got my name because my parents knew they were moving here when I was born."

He got in on the other side, and after we were both settled, he drove us out of the guesthouse. Once we were slowly making our way to the main road, he briefly turned to me, his expression curious. "Really? Were your parents working here?"

"Yeah, they moved here a few months after they got married, in 1990. They came to work with Children International. After the food crisis, you know?"

He nodded at my words, but the smile that had been on his face was replaced with a grimace as he started the car. "Many people working with international organizations came here once those photos of starving children were seen around the world. Unfortunately, for too many people, that is still all they care to know about our country."

I sighed in agreement, certain that if I hadn't been personally connected, I'd probably be one of those who made all kinds of uninformed assumptions. "My parents were captivated with this place from the moment they arrived. They were only here for a year that first time. But they came back in '94, after I was born. My dad was pretty set on me having an Ethiopian name, and Desta it was. He loved this place."

Elias's smile made a reappearance, and this one was radiant, like it pleased him to no end that my dad was infatuated with his country. "I like that story. Sounds like your father has a strong soul. He knows how special our country is, and not everyone can feel that."

I gulped, almost sad I had to tell him. "He died, my dad. When I was in high school."

His face grew serious, and when he turned to me, his eyes were so full of sympathy I felt like crying. "I'm sorry to hear that. It must have been very hard to lose your father so young."

I looked out the window and exhaled loudly, once again bemused at the onslaught of mixed emotions I'd been hit with since I'd arrived. "Yeah, it was hard." After all these years, whenever the death of my father came up, my usual answer was aimed more at trying to make the other person less uncomfortable. But here in the half-light of the Ethiopian dawn, for some reason, I felt like I could say the truth. "It still is hard, but we got through it. My mom loved living here too. She's so excited I'm here."

He exhaled at my words, and I was surprised to find I didn't shrink at Elias's reaction. It didn't feel like pity—it felt like he was trying to hold space for me to feel what I needed to.

He gave me a few moments, and when he spoke, it was back to the business at hand. "Then we must not let you down. First stop today is to get the best coffee in town."

I was grateful to him for changing the subject—it was like he could sense I didn't have the energy for this much emotion right now.

I smiled, shaking my head. "Wow, that must be something. I've already had pretty amazing coffee, and I don't think any of the places were particularly special."

He nodded, listening as he drove through the busy streets. "We'll go to Kaldi's—they have breakfast and coffee there. All farenji love that place." He straightened his back, like I'd just challenged him to blow me away with this cup of coffee. "I think it's because the logo and colors are similar to Starbucks in the States."

I laughed, now really eager to see this place. "Oh, really? Like they copied it or something?"

"Well…" He kept his eyes trained on the road, and I wished I could see his face more clearly, because I was pretty sure there was a dimple happening. "I think they might have borrowed the idea a bit *too* closely. I heard Starbucks requested they make changes to it, and they did." He lifted his right hand, index and finger close together. "Now it's a bit similar, but not too much. I've never been to the U.S., but all the visitors say the coffee here is a lot better." He lifted a hand to point at the parking lot of a very busy-looking café. "We're almost there, so you can judge for yourself."

I looked at him askance and tried hard to not grin at the level of seriousness this coffee talk had gotten. "It'll be better. Like I said, every cup of coffee I've had in Addis so far has been next-level delicious. I had like, five macchiatos yesterday. It's probably why I couldn't sleep."

He did turn around then, just a flash of teeth and happy man, which after only twenty minutes was already enough to weaken my defenses.

The crush was inevitable at this point.

"Yes, farenji always go a little overboard with the coffee at first. Don't worry, I'll remind you to switch to tea if you have too many."

I flashed him my own smile this time. "Thanks. I need help when it comes to resisting the siren song of caffeine."

He gave me a look that was equal parts side-eye and genuine empathy. "Our coffee can be hard to resist."

I gulped and looked out the window again, because now I was feeling things just from the guy using the words *hard to resist*.

I pulled myself together as we walked into the café, and started taking in the place. I expected a small storefront like the others I'd been to, but this place was huge. It could seat at least fifty people, and it was buzzing. It looked more like a café you'd find in Italy than the States. There were murals all over the walls with maps of the different coffee-producing regions in the country. The colors of the store were the yellow, green, and red of the Ethiopian flag. The floors were gleaming white marble and there was a lot of dark wood, chrome, and glass. Most of the tables were filled with young men and women. And there were servers walking around delivering coffee, pastries, and what looked like multilayered fruit smoothies in tall, skinny glasses. The smell of fresh roasted coffee beans was mouthwatering.

When we got closer to the service counter, I finally got a good look at the logo. I grinned at the familiar green-and-white circle, but at the center, instead of the mermaid, was a small coffee cup surrounded by the precious Ethiopian coffee beans. I pointed at it to get Elias's attention. "It's slightly similar, but definitely not the same."

It took him a second, but when he realized I was referring to the logo, that ever-present smile came out again. "Yes, no mermaid for us. Our magic is in the coffee."

"This is true," I agreed, charmed with him and the unapologetic pride he clearly felt.

"What would you like?" Elias asked as he gestured toward a hand-painted menu above the counter, and I realized he was offering to buy me breakfast.

I shook my head and slid my hand in my pocket for my wallet. "No, I can get it..."

His expression was serious, and he directed a short but very firm shake of his head at me. "No. Desta, I will pay for breakfast. Please."

Where did that dip in my stomach come from? This wasn't a fucking brunch date. I was working. My lack of self-preservation seemed to be reaching new levels on this trip. Still, I caved. "I'll have the egg and cheese croissant."

Holy shit, that smile and those dancing eyes were like kryptonite. I almost swooned from the way he was looking at me. He rubbed his palms together like I'd given him the best news he'd heard all week. "Eshi, Desta."

"All right, you win, but I'm buying next time," I said, feigning annoyance, and made a show of pouting and crossing my arms over my chest, eliciting a grin from Elias.

While he took care of our order, I looked around. There were a lot of what looked like students or young professionals, some dressed very fashionably. Not exactly what I would call American fashion, but a mash-up between European and hipster styles. Other than a group that could have been South Asian, everyone else was Ethiopian.

I turned back to Elias to ask him a question, but he was focused on his phone. I waited for him in silence, still exploring the place. I noticed that some patrons ordered in a mix of Amharic and English. I thought about the Spanglish I'd grown up speaking at home, and it occurred to me that when I was here as a baby, Amharic had been in the mix too.

We sat down to wait for our orders. When the server brought the food I saw that Elias's drink came in a clear glass coffee cup, and I couldn't tell what it was. The bottom two-thirds of the cup had a clear amber-colored liquid, but the top looked like very dark coffee. "What is that?"

Elias worked on spooning quite a bit of sugar in the mysterious drink before pushing it toward me. "It's a Spris, half coffee and half tea. I order it so I can drink more and still be able to sleep. Habesha love their bunna and chai breaks, and I can end up drinking too much caffeine if I don't watch it. As you already found out, Desta."

Oh man, winking.

Sexy winks were not going to be good for me.

I cleared my throat in another weak attempt to keep it together. "Interesting. I'll try that next time."

Another wink. Yep. I was in trouble.

I tried to regroup and went with a topic that wouldn't lead us down a path that risked more appearances of the dimple, or more winking with perfectly lashed brown eyes. "So how long have you been working for *Aid USA*? Do you like it?" I asked, holding back a whimper after taking a second sip of my incredibly delicious macchiato.

Elias swirled his spoon, trying to dissolve all the sugar he put in his very short cup of tea/coffee as he talked. "About five years. I got the driver job while I was still in university." He talked as he took careful sips. He licked his bottom lip every time, and I needed to find another spot on his face to focus on, because this was going to end poorly.

"So you worked full time while in school? That's a lot."

He shrugged, fiddling with the cutlery the server had brought us. "I went to Addis Ababa University, and their classes are very demanding. I didn't really work the first three years, but I got this job the last year." This time he ran his tongue over the little spoon. Oh God.

I nodded, trying hard to focus on what he was saying, but it was a struggle.

"I wanted to do an online master's degree from a school in the UK right after I finished my B.A., and the embassy jobs pay well. I also had a lot of time to read in between drives," he said, smiling. "And they helped with school, which is nice. The logistics coordinator position is interesting too."

There was something in how he said that made me want to ask more questions.

"That's great." I knew in a lot of the places I'd worked in, U.S. Embassy positions, even service ones, were coveted because of the pay and benefits. I also knew of colleagues in other countries who took jobs that were completely unrelated to their actual degrees because the pay was better. "What's your degree in? Did you enroll in the master's program?" I asked, genuinely interested.

Something in his demeanor changed with my questions, and when he looked at me, it was different. He was really looking at me now. I thought the Elias of the past thirty minutes would be a problem, but this intensity was enough to set my insides on fire. "In psychology, and yes, I did. I finished it this past May. The master's was in cultural psychology, actually."

"Oh, that's great. Tell me about it," I encouraged as I worked on my breakfast.

He seemed unsure, like he couldn't quite believe I wanted to hear about his degree, but after a second he conceded. "I'm interested in studying the psychological effects of colonization in Eastern Africa. Particularly masculinity, misogyny, and how that's impacted our social constructs around gender."

Whoa.

"What exactly are you looking at?" I asked, my food suspended in the air as I waited for his answer.

"Are you sure you want hear about it?" He cocked his head to the side, again hitting me with a piercing look. He was sizing me up. Figuring out if I was really interested, or just humoring him.

"Absolutely," I said honestly, and boy, was I unprepared for what happened next.

Elias leaned in, those brown eyes focused on my face, his body primed to unleash all the words he was holding inside. When he spoke, the passion there almost knocked me over.

"Ethiopia was never colonized, although we were occupied by Italy in the 1930s," he explained before continuing, "and even though East Africa wasn't impacted by the transatlantic slave trade as West Africa was, the brutalities of colonization were felt far and wide here. It changed the course of our history in so many ways."

For an instant, I wondered if he was about to get loud and preachy. But instead he grabbed his cup again and spoke in a low but serious voice. "I'd like to look into how that collective trauma has impacted our concept of masculinity, and how it factors into violence against women and children. Along the lines of the work of Frantz Fanon." He looked at me intensely, clearing his throat, then smiled ruefully. "Sorry, this is not exactly light conversation. It can be heavy."

"Not at all." He gave me a look that clearly said *yeah, right*, but I insisted, "I'm serious. My best friend Lucía is a big fan of Fanon—she gave me *The Wretched of the Earth* to read in college, and it sort of blew my mind."

His face brightened at that, but he stood up after sipping the last of his tea. "We can talk more in the car." This was not a man who let his responsibilities fall by the wayside just to hear himself talk, and of course that only made my infatuation go up a notch. "We should get on the road if we want to get to Awassa by early afternoon. We'll stop for lunch in Lake Langano. There's a nice place there. They have good fish—you can't go to the Rift Valley and not eat Nile perch."

I stood up after making sure I drank every last drop of my macchiato. "Sounds great. I love fish, and I'm looking forward to seeing the lakes."

He gave me that grin I noticed came out whenever I showed excitement in the things I wanted to see or do while I was here. I had to be careful not to read into it too much, though. From my own experience with Ethiopian friends, and the hundreds of stories I had heard from my parents, I knew they were immensely proud of their homeland and their history. Maybe that was all this was, not some special thing going on between me and Elias.

* * *

ONCE IN THE CAR, we navigated the roads heading out of Addis Ababa, which even at six thirty in the morning were starting to get pretty busy. Driving in Addis was a cacophony of color and sound. There were people everywhere: cars, blue-and-white taxi vans, eighteen-wheelers, SUVs of every make and year imaginable, and motorcycles going in all directions.

Like many a developing country I'd been in, I noticed Ethiopians could get creative with their vehicle passengers. We drove past a motorcycle with three riders, except in between the first and second guy was what looked like a live sheep.

"Nice," I said, pointing to the threesome. "I've seen chickens on motorcycles before, but never a sheep."

Elias looked at me with amused eyes. "Farenjis are always surprised by that. How are they supposed to get the sheep home after buying it at the market?"

"True." He had a point. "So, remind me were farenji comes from? I mean, it sort of sounds like foreigner."

"It's always been the word used to describe someone from outside of Ethiopia. I think it comes from the Arabic word 'farenji.' And you're correct, it does mean 'foreigner.'"

I leaned back in my seat as we talked, already feeling way too comfortable with Elias. "I'm glad I'm fulfilling the expected behavior, at least so far. Anything else on the list I should make sure I do while I'm here? I don't want to disappoint."

My tone was teasing, and from the way his mouth turned up, I could tell Elias totally got my joke. "Well, lots of farenji want to go and eat kitfo—it's raw beef with spices, like steak tartare. They always say if they take medicine, they won't get sick from eating it. They take the medicine and still get sick. That happens a lot." He shook his head in amused confusion as I chuckled.

"I can assure you that won't be me. I don't eat beef. I guess I'll just get drunk and try to speak in bad Amharic."

He let out a laugh at that, his deep voice full of humor when he spoke. "This also happens a lot."

Oh man, he was so sexy.

Elias drove us through a particularly tricky intersection, and I used the quiet moment to take him in. He was wearing a gray fleece with the Aid USA logo on the breast pocket, and a thick leather bracelet watch that made his hands look like a warrior's or something. He was also perfectly groomed. The nails of his strong hands were clipped and buffed, like he'd had a manicure. He was clean-shaven, but his hair was long enough that he needed to pull it back with an elastic band. It looked like a halo of tight curls around his head.

I realized that I'd been staring for way longer than could be considered polite, and turned my attention to looking out the window and getting familiar with the place I'd been tied to from before birth. Addis had seen an economic boom in the last fifteen years and the city was expanding, but as we got farther out, we saw less concrete.

An hour into the drive, we began passing mountains and green hills, each stretching as far as the eye could see. We also passed vendors by the side of the road. Women with babies strapped to their backs sat by tables full of huge honeycombs or bottles of water. I even spotted a few roadside artists.

It was beautiful, all of it. The sky was so big here. Huge boulders dotted the landscape, and occasionally we would see patches of flowering cacti lining the road.

Once it looked like we had gotten past the heavier traffic, Elias turned to me. "Do you want to put on some music? I have a cord here if you have your phone."

"Are you sure?" I asked, not wanting to subject him to my music. "We can play what you like, since you're the one driving. I'm pretty open—I'll listen to anything. *If* it's good." I winked.

He chuckled at my attempt at humor. "I have very particular music taste. You may not like it."

"Uh-huh. So tell me, what do you listen to?"

He gave me a look, and I knew he was a messing with me when he burst out laughing, "Actually, I can't stop listening to Beyoncé lately!"

For some reason that made laugh too, "Hey, nothing wrong with Queen Bey. *Lemonade* is epic."

At my words he turned serious and said, "I usually listen to a lot of blues and jazz, but that album is amazing. I think she tells a beautiful story." He shook his head as I stared at him, once again bowled over by him. "Now I've made the whole thing too serious. No way will it live up to this introduction. Let's hear some music you like."

"Okay, but for the record, I could listen to *Lemonade* anytime," I said as I got my iPhone out.

Knowing I'd be offline a lot during my trips outside of Addis, I'd downloaded a ton of music, podcasts, and audiobooks on my phone, so I had lots of choices. For some reason, being on this open road with what seemed like a never-ending range of mountains made me want to listen to something a bit melancholy.

I hit play and "Poison & Wine" came in through the speakers. I immediately felt the music affect me. The contrasting pulse of the guitar and light piano, like two heartbeats skittering in unison, wreaked havoc on my recently bruised heart. This playlist was one of my favorites to listen to while driving. But today, I felt exposed listening to it with Elias. Like he'd somehow figure out my sad love story.

Next to me, he grunted approval of the music. "I like this song," he said, tapping the steering wheel. "Their voices are so perfect together."

I smiled and turned to look at him. "The Civil Wars."

He made another sound of approval at the name of the band, and we listened to the rest of the song in silence.

When it was over, I saw his jaw clench for a second, clearly thinking hard on whatever he was about to say. When he spoke, his voice was low, like he wasn't totally sure it was a good idea. "The love in that song is the kind which can only survive if it's tearing you apart or putting you back together."

Damn. Drag me, Elias.

I had no idea how to respond to that. I sat there in silence, thinking of what he'd said, how exposed it made me feel, when I noticed Elias bopping his head, his dark brown curls bouncing as he sang around a big grin on his face. I turned my attention to the music and noticed the Civil Wars cover of "Billie Jean" was playing. I'd forgotten about that one. But I was extremely charmed by Elias's obvious delight.

"MJ!" he crowed, his shoulders now moving to the music.

He swiveled his head, emulating Michael, and started singing along a bit faster than the version from the Civil Wars. Before I could overthink it, I started to sing along too, the intensity of the previous moment left behind.

We belted out the lyrics as we drove through the Ethiopian countryside, and for the first time since I'd landed, I thought this trip might have been exactly what I needed.

CHAPTER 3

We listened to the rest of the playlist, singing along when the inspiration hit us, and when it finished, Elias turned to me for a second. "You're our official DJ now. Do you have more music from them?"

I shook my head regretfully, already finding it hard to deny Elias anything. "Nope, they stopped making music together a few years ago. Sounds like they didn't get along."

His face turned serious again. "Sometimes, creating something so beautiful it ends up using up all the joy you get from it."

"Yeah," I said with a sigh, feeling once again like everything Elias said seemed to come from some deep and wise place. Every word deliberate. It was unnerving. I didn't think I could handle that level of depth if the conversation veered toward me. I sank into the seat of the car, considering what he'd said, and it hurt a little.

I'd never made anything beautiful with someone else. I was always so eager to "make a connection." So busy finding ways to be noticed or liked by others that I forgot to think about whether we were even a good match. Exhibit A was the disaster with my ex, Miguel.

We'd met at a bar in DC just a few weeks after he'd started a master's program at American University. I'd been working at Aid USA headquarters. He was smart, funny, and sexy as hell, and I fell fast. But it wasn't just the sex. Not for me, at least. He was also Dominican, and we'd talked for hours on end about our common roots.

Being born and raised all over the world, I'd always been fascinated by mother's homeland. She had a complicated relationship with her country. We never really visited, and she wasn't very close to her family, but she loved it, and spoke of it passionately. Even now, almost forty years after leaving the DR to go the States for school, she'd still cry when certain songs that reminded her of home came on the radio.

Miguel, on the other hand, did not do complicated. He'd come to the States for school, but loved his life in the DR. I never stopped to think that meant he was just having a bit of fun with me, and never planned to stick around. When I asked him what we'd been doing for the past two years, he'd looked at me in astonishment and said, "Fucking."

And in the end, he was right. He'd never promised me anything. He constantly talked about how much he missed his comfortable upper-middle-class life in the DR. How he could go back to a job that paid him enough to live like a king, while in the States he would have to do the grind like everyone else.

I mean, yeah, he was a two-timing bastard who kept his girlfriend in the DR on the side the whole time we dated. But I'd had every opportunity to see the writing on the wall. To notice he just nodded distractedly whenever I talked about the future. I'd ignored all of it and pressed on. I didn't even have the strength to hate him now. I was too fucking exhausted from carrying our relationship single-handedly for two years.

That train of thought put me back in a funk, and to make things worse, I started feeling guilty about not emailing Lucía to let her know I got in okay. I had to call her tonight or tomorrow morning because she was probably ready to roll out the search party.

I tried to get out of my head and turned to Elias, who'd been driving and listening to the Bob Marley playlist I'd switched to while I'd brooded. "Hey? Is it seven or eight hours' difference to the East

Coast? I know there's a change during Daylight Savings Time, but I can't remember how it goes."

"We're eight hours ahead of DC. We always have to keep that straight, since we have so many people travelling through here from headquarters. Sometimes they've been to so many countries in a single trip they have no idea what time zone they're in when they arrive."

I nodded, relating strongly to that feeling. "I've been there, and thanks." I grabbed my phone, ready to switch up the music if he wanted something different. "Are you okay with this, or do you want me to change it?"

He shook his head and smiled, facing the road. "I can always listen to Bob."

I could not argue with that. "Me too."

After a moment he spoke again. "We'll stop for lunch at Lake Langano soon. It's one of the bigger lakes in the Rift Valley, and there are a few hotels around it with nice restaurants."

I nodded excitedly, grateful for the distraction. "I can't wait. I've been reading about the lakes. What kind of Nile perch should I get at the restaurant?"

"Fish goulash," he said in a tone that brooked no argument. Elias certainly knew what he liked.

"Like the soup?" I asked in surprise.

He lifted a shoulder, his face amused. "It's more like fried fish in a tomato-based sauce, which you eat with injera." The *of course* was left unsaid, and I found myself grinning again.

"Naturally, it would involve injera," I deadpanned, eliciting a sexy laugh. "But why goulash? That isn't an Amharic word. Also, more injera is fine with me. I could eat it all day, every day."

He laughed again, still focused on the road. "I'm not sure where goulash came from, but that's what it's been called since I can remember." He took his eyes off the road for a second and turned to me, that teasing expression on his face. "If you can eat that much injera, then you really are a Habesha baby."

"I told you I am," I said. He winked again, then took his hand off the wheel to move the gearshift. I could do was stare. A limb fixation was definitely a cry for help, and yet here we were.

In an effort not to embarrass myself further, I attempted more small talk. "So does your family miss you when you're out of town working in the field? Or do you live alone?"

He shook his head. "No, most young people here live with their parents and family until they get married. I'm twenty-eight, and technically could afford to be on my own, but I live with my parents, and my sister and her family." He cleared his throat like he was considering what else to say. "That way I can save and help with the house expenses. But they're used to my schedule."

He used that same tone from before, like there was more to the story, but I was not going to get pushy. Well, pushier. "How about a girlfriend? Does she mind your schedule?"

Totally not pushy. Was I intentionally trying to get to the point where he asked me about *my* girlfriend, and I'd have to lie or say something that could make this trip incredibly uncomfortable? Did my shame at being an intrusive shit keep me from staring at him like I needed an answer ASAP?

Nope.

Elias just shook his head and simply said, "No girlfriend to worry about."

The way his throat moved and shoulders tensed when he answered made me veer off from my line of questioning. I decided to just let that shit go and not plant any more conversational bombs for now.

* * *

WE GOT to Awassa in the midafternoon, and after a quick check-in at the hotel, we went to our rooms with the plan to meet with the others for dinner.

The hotel had great internet, and though it was early morning in New York, I decided to try Luce. She would probably be getting home from a shift at the hospital and be around for a quick chat. I video-

Skyped her and she connected after only a couple of rings. I grinned as soon as I saw her pissed-off face filling up my laptop screen.

"You little fucker! I thought you were dead!" she yelled, then sucked her teeth as I sat there cheesing. Acting like she was so pissed she wanted to snatch me right through the screen was my best friend's love language.

I wasn't stupid enough to say it, though. So I teased her instead. "I love you too, Luce."

That got me an epic eye roll. "Would it have killed you to send a two-word text? 'I'm fucking alive' would've worked."

"Uh, that's three words, genius," I said, certain that would just set her off on another rant about how I was going to be the death of her.

God, it was good to see her face.

From where she was sitting I could see the back of her leather couch, which she'd saved for like, six months to buy. Behind her were rows and rows of books in white bookshelves. Her curls were an unruly mess, and she was wearing a T-shirt that said *Flexin' in my Complexion*. I could see her Kindle and a huge cup of coffee, probably decaf, sitting in front on the table.

Luce and I had met the first day of ninth grade the fall after my dad died. After he passed away my mom decided to move to Ithaca in Upstate New York, where my dad's parents lived. We'd always been close to them, and back then she needed the support.

Lucía's family lived just two streets away from us. We were both only children, and hung onto each other for dear life through everything. Her parents were also one of the few Dominican families in Ithaca, which sealed the friendship between us. We both stayed in town for college, but after graduation Luce went to Seattle to get her master's in nursing and later settled in New York City. In the four years since we'd finished college, I'd used DC as my home base, though I was barely there. After years of living so far apart, these Skype sessions were old hat for us.

Lucía was my best friend and I loved her, but she never, ever sugarcoated the truth. Which made me reluctant to share my instant fixation on Elias. I *was* kind of embarrassed, because I'd known the man for a day. I had no idea what kind of person he was, and I had basically turned into a cliché.

"Ayo!" I jumped, startled by Lucía's voice. I must have been doing my "in my feelings face" as she called it, because she tilted her head and stared at me with a frown before asking, "You call me and then just sit there in silence. Did something happen? Are things not working out with the job?"

I shook myself, trying to act normal before she caught on. "Everything's fine. It's been great so far, actually. This place is amazing," I said, running my hands over my hair, feeling exposed again. "It's so weird being here as an adult and on my own, because some things feel so familiar. I know I couldn't possibly remember much from when I was a baby, or even from when I was six and we were here for those few months, you know?" I confessed, genuinely puzzled by the jumble of emotions that had been coursing through me from the moment I stepped off the plane.

"I bet," Luce said, still looking at me like she wasn't sure how to read my mood. "It's got to be wild in many ways, and sad in others. Especially because your mom always speaks of her times there like they were the best years of her life. It's sad that she doesn't feel up for a visit while you're there. Speaking of which, have you called her?" She gave me a pointed look, like she already knew the answer.

"I haven't," I said, hanging my head. "I will first thing tomorrow, though! I need to be in the right frame of mind. You know how she is. She gets so worked up and cries and shit. I'm not ready for all that yet."

She put her hands up. "Hey, I get it. I've got *two* Dominicans on my ass with the guilt trip every time we talk." she said it, raising two fingers up to the screen. "I don't blame you."

I laughed at the exasperation on her face, like her parents hadn't been like that her entire life.

"You must be a ball of feelings, sweetie, but I'm glad you're liking it. Tell me about the people. Have you met anyone cool? Is the coffee beyond?"

I swooned, already fantasizing about the macchiato I was getting as soon as I ended the call. "Oh man, the coffee really is amazing. I may have to start setting down hard and fast rules around amount consumed per day, because at this rate I may permanently injure myself with caffeine." She rolled her eyes at my strung-out expression.

I took a moment before answering her second question, thinking of how to proceed. "I haven't met that many people yet. Just the woman who'll be my boss, and she's really cool. The co-worker I rode down with today is pretty nice." I coughed, averting my eyes. "Very interesting."

She smiled, completely innocent to my extremely bad choices. "How is he interesting?"

"Well, I don't know that much about him, really." Not because my nosy ass hadn't tried. "But he's a psychologist—cultural psychology, actually. He's looking into how colonization impacts the collective psyche." Her eyes widened with genuine interest. "He's really into Frantz Fanon."

She *really* perked up at that. This was the type of stuff she loved. "Whoa, that's some majorly woke shit right there. That *is* interesting. A bit intense, but hey." She lifted a shoulder and gulped from her huge mug. "You don't mind intense."

"I don't, and he *is* kind of intense, not in a bad way though. We were listening to some music on the drive and he got incredibly deep about 'Poison & Wine' by the Civil Wars. I mean, all of their songs are like, life or death good, but still."

Luce made a sound of approval and nodded. "Yep, they're bomb." Then her face got all sad. "I still get bummed out when I think about them breaking up."

"Yeah." I sighed, and for some incomprehensible reason, asked the last thing I should be asking. "So, have you heard from Miguel?"

This was not a question that would go over well. I averted my eyes to a spot over her head as soon as the words came out of my mouth. I knew Lucía had him on her shit list forever and would (a) not pick up the phone if he did call, and (b) not tell me because she knew it wouldn't lead anywhere good.

The eye roll and growl she proffered confirmed I knew exactly who I was dealing with. "That come mierda knows not to dial my number. God, just thinking of that fuckface makes me mad." She ran her tongue over her front teeth, probably envisioning throat punching him, and crossed her arms over her chest. "What's he gonna call me for? Besides, I assume he's too busy planning his country club wedding in Santo Domingo with that skank he's engaged to."

"Come on, Luce," I said, trying to keep a straight face. "We don't really know she's a skank."

"Whatever. He's an asshole and I'm glad you're like, twenty countries away and getting all that drama out of your system. You deserve someone who worships and *sees* you and your beautiful heart. Not that trifling asshole." She twisted her mouth to the side, like even the thought of him left a bad taste. "No dick is that good."

I groaned at *that* hard truth. "Agreed. His wasn't, at least. And you just say that because I'm your favorite."

"You better believe it." Her expression was a mix of affection and worry. I knew she thought I'd spend the entire time I was here moping about Miguel. But it all seemed so distant now. Maybe he'd been right, and none of it had been that deep after all.

I looked back at Luce and noticed her eyes were getting droopy. When she yawned, she gave me a rueful look. "Babe, I gotta go. I'm about to keel over. I'm glad you got in all right and already have a potential friend. Love you and talk soon, okay?"

I cringed internally at the mention of my new "friend" and blew her a kiss before signing off.

As I opened up the documents I wanted to review before our dinner meeting, I considered what I was feeling. I'd left DC feeling numb and lost, and now that I was here, I felt...different. Before getting on the plane to Addis Ababa, I'd been wondering if I even wanted to do this work. Never mind the acceptance to the NYU social work master's program for the fall, I'd been avoiding thinking about. All that was still up in the air.

Yeah, I was still lost, unsure about what I'd do next, but that numbness had turned into something more like anticipation. I tried not to probe the source of it too much because I knew it probably had to do with my ill-advised crush on a certain logistics coordinator, and that was not advisable in any sort of way.

* * *

DINNER WAS a long and serious affair since we had a lot to prepare before our first survey day. By the time I got to my room it was past ten, but as tired as I was, sleep would not come. The hotel room had mosquito nets on the beds, and the ceiling fan made it flutter. It felt like there were birds flying over my head, and that, plus the lingering jet lag, made it hard to settle down.

After half an hour of tossing and turning, I gave up on sleep and decided to go out and take a walk around the hotel compound. They had a nice garden and pool area, and I hoped the fresh air would help me relax. As I stepped out of my room, I shivered in the cold night air, looking up at the sky.

It was magnificent.

Of all the places I'd been to, this sky seemed to have the most stars. They looked so close, too. I felt like I could reach out and touch them. A wave of emotion hit me as I stood there with my face raised to the night sky. Unbidden, a tear rolled down my cheek as I thought about my parents. Had they been to this hotel when they lived here? Had they taken walks in this same garden together? As I struggled to recall my father's face, the frantic fear that one day I'd completely forget him resurfaced, making my heart gallop in my chest. The truth was that every year my memories of him dimmed a little more, but here I felt connected to him in a way I hadn't in a long time.

I heard someone approach, so I quickly brushed my tears away and turned to see Elias walking toward me. He was wearing a thicker bright orange fleece this time, and the contrast of that fiery color against his brown skin made me a little breathless.

"Jet lag?" he called out to me as he approached.

I nodded and walked over to meet him halfway. "Yeah, I'm still all out of whack. What're you still doing up?"

He shrugged as he looked up at the sky. "I couldn't sleep. When I drive all day, my body takes some time to slow down. I like to take a walk before bed."

"Well, we can keep each other company while we try to summon the sleep gods."

The sleep gods? Who the hell talked like that?

He just smiled and kept walking with me as I hurried to make small talk. "I assume going for a run in the morning won't be an issue?" I asked with a smirk, expecting him to make some comment about Ethiopian runners and their greatness.

"Of course. There'll be people out there starting at dawn. We're serious about our running in this part of the world." He winked, and a swell of butterflies swerved inside my chest. "It's easier to run here too; the air isn't as thin as Addis's."

I nodded at his statement. Not being up seven thousand feet *would* make it less treacherous to go for a run.

Elias lifted his hand as he gave me directions. "You just make a left when you get out to the road and keep going until the roundabout, then come back. The whole loop is about three miles. I run that way when I'm here."

"Perfect." I wanted to ask if he'd go with me, but I just thanked him instead, and kept walking at his side.

Elias seemed so at peace. Unhurried. So unlike my own approach to life. But wasn't that what I was looking for here? To take stock, to find a new way to coexist with myself that didn't involve erasing my needs and wants to keep those around me happy?

Usually when I met someone I couldn't stop talking, trying to impress them, or sound smart or knowledgeable. But with Elias I felt it would be pointless. Like he'd know it was just noise.

"I might see you out there." His rough voice in the silent night brought me back from my wayward thoughts.

"Sure, sounds good," I answered, trying not to sound too eager.

"I have to get the vehicle ready first thing since we'll be driving rough for a good part of the day. But if I get up early enough, I'll have time for a short run." When I looked up, I was greeted with that warm smile he always seemed to have for me.

But when I got closer, I realized he looked tired. "Do you need help getting the car ready? I can skip the run and help out."

He looked surprised by that. "Thank you for offering, but the other drivers can help. It will be a long day, but you'll get to see some very nice parts of Gedeo, at least."

I rubbed my hands together, feeling excited for the work ahead. "I'm looking forward to it—it's been a while since I've actually done field work. These days I mostly go the main country offices to do my stuff."

For this job, we were collecting data to assess a nutrition program for children in rural areas who were under the age of five. Aid USA had been running it in partnership with the Ethiopian government. We'd be in the field most of the time.

"Rain has been over for a few months, so it shouldn't be too hard to get to the more remote villages," Elias said as we walked.

"That's good," I answered, lost in thought over the conditions we'd find.

Many families in the rural areas of the country still relied on subsistence farming, so if there was a bad year in the fields, there was just not enough food to go around. A lot of people depended on this program, and with the current political environment in the States, Aid USA officials were feeling the pressure to justify a few more years of funding. Our job was to collect information they'd use to make their case.

We made our way through the hotel grounds until we came to an enclosed patio, and Elias pointed at a semi-hidden bench by a hedge of jasmine. When we sat, I could feel Elias's body heat even from a couple of inches away. I glanced down, trying to focus on anything other than how close we were. When I looked at his feet, I noticed he'd taken off his work boots and was wearing black Birkens. His toes were thick on the top and very long, and he had a mole below his big toe that looked like a small coffee bean.

He noticed I was looking his toes, then curled them in, smiling self-consciously. "They're very strange-looking. Too big."

"I was looking at your coffee bean," I said, pointing at his foot.

He laughed and wiggled them again. "You're not the first one to notice." He kept looking at me for another moment and surprised me with a question. "Are you sure you're all right?" he asked, obviously picking up on my gloomy mood.

"It's weird, but even though I'm missing my dad more since I got here than I have in years, it feels different. Better," I said, and it sounded like a question. "Like it's a wound I've been keeping covered and clean, but what it needed to heal was air and sun." I shook my head at my rambling. "That makes no sense."

His face turned serious. "You make sense to me."

I frowned at how he phrased that and wondered if something had been lost in translation. But the way his kind, dark brown eyes were set on my face made me dismiss the thought. He moved a little closer, and his curls were almost brushing my cheek. I wished I could tip my face up to him, wanting to feel his touch on my bare skin with an urgency that startled me.

He spoke into the quiet night. "Just because something isn't festering does not mean it's healed."

I nodded, then turned my face away again when he looked at me like he wanted to ask more questions. Before he could I stood, doing my best to shake off the intensity of the last few minutes. "I think I'm going to turn in. See you in the morning."

He dipped his head and stood in silence, pointing in the opposite direction of my room. "I'm over there."

We parted ways then, but as I walked up the pathway, I could feel the weight of Elias's stare all the way to my door.

CHAPTER 4

The sky was starting to lighten when the call to prayer from a nearby mosque woke me the next morning. My job had taken me to a lot of different places, so I was used to music or prayers rousing villages. This muezzin had a particularly melodic voice, and I lay in bed, drifting in the cadence of his chanting as I thought of the day ahead.

We'd be going deeper into the rural parts of the region today, and I was looking forward to that. Being out in the field and talking to women, men, and children was always enriching and humbling for me.

It's hard to explain to someone who hasn't seen it just how little people have in some parts of the world. No electricity, no running water, homes made of hay and clay, at times not much to eat. A few changes of clothes for each person in a family, and if they were lucky, more than one pair of shoes. Still, they proudly opened their scrupulously cared-for homes, and generously offered what they had to eat or drink.

I was excited to do the job I'd been given over the next few weeks. And maybe, if I was honest, I was also looking forward to spending the day stuck in a car with Elias. I wasn't ready to give my reckless crush free rein yet, but I was totally giving myself a pass on "getting to know him because he seemed interesting."

I took the end of the call to prayer as my cue get out of bed, and within minutes I was walking out of my room. I warmed up a bit by the pool and left the hotel compound at a leisurely jog. The sun was almost fully up over the misty fields as I ran past. It was such a sight that I had to stop and look. The horizon went on forever here, which made for a stunning sunrise. I watched it in a reverent silence until I felt chilled and had to move.

I set off on the path Elias recommended with Cardi B for a sound-track, the movement and bite of the morning air kick-starting my jet lagged brain. About two-thirds through the loop I began to sense some runners behind me. When I looked over my shoulder, I saw five or six boys of various ages grinning at me as they tried to catch up. I took my eye off the path too long and lost my footing for a second, then decided to give them a real run for their money. I ripped out my earbuds and took off back to the hotel as fast as I could go. They all shrieked, seemingly delighted at the challenge, and ran after me.

I lost most of my running companions along the way, but two of them kept up with me. I was almost ready to give up and let them pass me when I saw Elias come up on my other side, grinning from ear to ear. He ran alongside me for a second and then panted out, "I forgot to mention that the local boys like to chase the farenjis who go out on runs. It's a big achievement to outrun them, you see."

I looked at him, but was too out of breath to say anything, and in a last-ditch effort I sprinted, leaving Elias in the dust too. I made it to the hotel, barely, and collapsed on the lawn. Elias ran in a bit after-ward, laughing hard as he dropped down next to me, and it wasn't long before the last two boys made it back as well. I turned to them, still gasping for breath, held up my finger, and hobbled to my room. I got a few Jolly Ranchers and packs of gum out of my bag to hand out to the kids. They plucked them from my hands with a thank you and ran off, throwing their fists up in the air, hollering in victory at their sullen friends who had finally caught up.

Elias just shook his head as we watched them run off. "By

tomorrow every boy in Awassa will know there's a farenji giving away candy in this hotel. You will be like the Pied Piper when you go out for runs."

I laughed and shook my head at the image of me with a trail of smiling boys running around town. "I only have a limited supply of candy, and I don't have an evil ploy to lure little children. I'm also not afraid to say no." I stuck my finger in the air to press my point. "And only those who can keep up with my lightning speed get the spoils."

He threw his head back and laughed at my preening. He was flushed and sweaty, and I really wanted to run my hand over his face and chest. I settled for teasing him a bit instead. "And the Pied Piper? That's a pretty Eurocentric analogy, sir."

He smiled ruefully at my callout, but lifted his shoulder as he answered. "If something works, I'll use it, *and…*" Now he was the one using a finger to make a point. "I *will* give the credit to whom it's due…a not-so Eurocentric approach."

"Touché," I agreed. Elias was quick on his feet, that was for sure. I was already half-addicted to these sharp exchanges with him. I had to be on my toes with this man. "I'm only half colonizer, though. My mother's from the Dominican Republic. It's—"

He interrupted me before I went on to my scripted DR history sound bite. "I know about Hispaniola. One side of the island is Dominican Republic and the other is Haiti, the first free Black republic in the world. Jean-Jacques Dessalines is a hero of mine." He smiled when he mentioned the Haitian general who led the slave rebellion in 1804.

"That's right." It never got old, connecting with someone over the pieces of who I was, which others rarely saw. Being biracial, I sometimes felt lost in an in-between world. I had to constantly make a space for myself where I didn't necessarily feel like I fit in. For Elias to not question my claim on Hispaniola brought the warm feeling in my chest back with a vengeance.

We stayed silent for a few minutes until he jumped up from the grass and pulled me to my feet. I realized then that other than shaking his hand when we met, I hadn't reached out to touch him at all. The warmth of his skin against mine made my stomach flutter. His eyes on me were intense, like he was trying to read every thought going through my head.

We looked at each other for another moment before he let go. Then he jerked his thumb over his shoulder, which I assumed indicated he was taking off. "I'm headed to shower and will grab a quick breakfast in the restaurant. Will you be ready to go in an hour?"

Right, plans for the day. For the job I was here to do, which didn't involve messing around with Elias in the yard of the hotel.

I nodded as I started turning away. "Yes. I told Sam I'd meet him for breakfast to go over plans, but it should be quick."

"Good. We should leave right at 8:00. We have to do a lot of driving today. I've also ordered some lunches and water bottles from the restaurant to take with us. There won't be places to stop on today's route."

I looked at the time on my watch and gave him a thumbs-up. "That gives me about forty-five minutes, which is more than enough. See you in a bit, and thanks for taking care of lunch."

I turned and started walking to my room. From the corner of my eye I saw Elias watching me, and his face had that intense look again.

Like I was something he was trying to figure out, but was afraid of the answers he'd discover.

* * *

I CAME downstairs to find Sam already in the dining room, leering at the woman sitting with him at the table. We'd met the day before, and he had been as much of a shithead as Bonnie has promised. Grateful that I didn't need to be stuck with him in a car all day, I walked over to them, bracing for whatever asinine thing would come out of his mouth. I'd only spent a few hours with him and was already completely over his frat bro posturing.

When I got to the table, I first turned to the woman and offered my hand. She was tall and slender, with beautiful golden-brown skin. Even in her jeans, hiking boots, and long-sleeved Aid USA T-shirt, she was stunning. I assumed this was our statistician, who had arrived late yesterday and had not made it to dinner.

"Hi, you must be Tsehay. I'm Desta."

She immediately stood up and grabbed my shoulder to do the double-kiss-and-embrace greeting that was compulsory for Ethiopians. My mother being Dominican, I was used to a kiss hello and goodbye, and after just a few days, I'd grown comfortable with the ritual. Ethiopians didn't wave or do hurried handshakes. No, a greeting was a moment of pause and connection that said "I want to show you how good it is to see you."

I responded to Tsehay's greeting in kind. She beamed at me as we pulled back. "You're like Habesha, Desta! With your name and such a proper greeting, you could fool anyone."

I laughed at how serious she seemed. "I'm glad you approve."

I turned to Sam, who had a puzzled look on his face, like he wasn't one hundred percent sure what my agenda was with Tsehay. I did my best to suppress my eye roll as I went to sit down across from him. "Hey Sam, how's it going?"

"Hey yourself." I was almost impressed by how he could make those two words sound like a full recrimination. "I was just going over the survey with Tsehay."

I glared at him, annoyed at his shitty pronunciation of her name. It was just *seh-high*, simple. Yet he somehow managed to butcher it. He'd done the same thing last night with some of the other team members we had dinner with.

"Just making sure she understands what we need to get out of the qualitative questions. We don't want people to give us their life story. Just what worked and what didn't about the program."

He then turned to Tsehay and started speaking in that annoying enunciated English that some Westerners used when talking to locals in developing countries. Hammering every single syllable to death and sounding out every vowel and consonant, like they were teaching kindergarteners the alphabet.

So fucking condescending.

For the next few minutes, I watched Tsehay listen to Sam drone on

39

with the mixture of weariness and boredom I'd seen on the faces of staff dealing with expats the world over. I could only feel for her, because as far as I knew, Tsehay was in the process of getting her doctoral degree in statistics. She'd also been working in the program we were surveying since the initial stages and was from this region, to boot. Why Sam thought he had to tell her how to ask questions to people she certainly knew how to speak to a hell of a lot better than he did, was a complete mystery to me.

When I couldn't stand it anymore I interrupted him, my voice as polite as I could make it in my uncaffeinated state. "Why don't we order some food before we start going over our plans, Sam?"

Without waiting for him to respond, I turned to Tsehay. "I would also like to get some input from you," I said, pulling out from my messenger bag the tablet we'd been using to do the surveys. "What would you like me to cover while I'm out with my team? I'm not new to this kind of work, but you're the expert here."

She gave me a look which was a mix between an eye roll and a hint of "at least one of these assholes has an ounce of sense."

We quickly ordered some food with Tsehay's assistance and started working out details. Turned out she was indeed an expert, and had not only helped run similar surveys, but was going to be my go-to in cleaning the data from the field before we passed it on to Sam. While we talked, he sat in a disgusted silence since he was no longer controlling the conversation.

After we finished, we rushed off for a final run to our rooms before heading to our vehicles. But as I was walking out, Sam stopped me and ground out, "I don't appreciate you undermining me in front of the local staff. I'm the monitoring and evaluation officer for this survey and I need to make sure I get the right information."

I just kept walking and didn't even bother looking at him when I responded. "How did I undermine you? I was letting Tsehay know I wanted to get her *expert* opinion on how to run a survey in this region. Of the three of us, she's the only person who's actually from here, not to mention a statistician. It makes sense to make sure she's on board with the plans for the day. Also, local staff is just staff, the same as you and me."

He just glared at me and scoffed. "Whatever. If this is your way of getting into her pants, there are ways to do it without fucking with my survey."

This time I did turn around so he could see I wouldn't let him talk to me—or about Tsehay—like that. "First of all," I said, holding a finger up close to his face. "It's not your survey, it's *Aid USA's* survey that *I'm* being paid to work on too. Second, if I wanted to get into anyone's pants I wouldn't be coming to you for advice. And third, I'm gay." I kept the "you fucking idiot" to myself, but just barely.

I spun around without waiting for his response. When I got to my door, I said as calmly as I could, "I hope you have a good day out there, Sam, and try to keep your assumptions to a minimum." He just glared at me before walking into his own room.

It only took me a few minutes to get my stuff ready, and I was down by our Land Cruiser before the agreed time. All the guys in our vehicle were there too, so I delivered some atrocious Amharic in an attempt to say hello before we all got into the vehicle. The guys thought I was hilarious, so at least that was something. Neither Abraham nor Yohannes spoke great English, but they would be there to help with the surveys in the regional language. So in addition to driving us all over to day, Elias would be serving as translator between the guys and me.

We quickly got into the truck, and as we headed towards the main road Elias called my name. I immediately reacted. It was like every cell in my body was on high alert around him. Everything in me aligned in his direction. "Yes?"

"We should be on the road to Dilla soon. Once we're on it, you can put the book on. Yohannes and Abraham both brought their headphones and said they'll listen to their own music."

I turned around to give the guys a thumbs-up before answering Elias. "Sounds good. Let me know and I'll start."

Last night at dinner I'd told Elias I had several audiobooks we could listen to while in the car. We would be on the road for many hours over the next five weeks, and he seemed pleased that we had a lot to choose from. He'd asked what book I wanted to listen to first, and in a moment of madness I'd blurted out *Aristotle and Dante Discover the Secrets of the Universe*. I hadn't read the book before, but I'd gotten it after Lucía recommended it. What I did know was that it was a young adult novel with two gay main characters, and I was feeling more than a bit anxious.

Elias seemed pretty laid back, but there was no way to tell how he would react once he realized what the book was about. I distracted myself by looking out the window. Everything was intensely green at this time of year, and as we drove, we passed the occasional mango or guava tree heavy with fruit. As we got farther into Gedeo, the area we'd be surveying, I noticed the dwellings looked different than the ones we'd seen on the way down from Addis.

"So are these houses traditional to the area? I know each tribe has its own style," I asked Elias.

He nodded, keeping his eyes on the road. "Yes, these are the Gedeo houses."

I looked out at the window at the homes dotting the lush green landscape. They looked almost like beehives: round on the bottom, but the roofs were cone-shaped and very tall. They were all surrounded by plants that looked like banana trees.

"Are those the false bananas?" I asked, aware that the plants were a major source of food for many tribes in Ethiopia.

Elias tipped his chin in the direction of a house on the left side of the road. "Eshi, that's ensete," he said snapping the syllables of the Amharic name for the plants. "They look just like a banana tree, but they don't bear fruit. We use the root to make bread."

I looked at some of the houses as we drove; they seemed to be built from bamboo and mud. "Right, I heard it's an important part of the diet here."

"We eat it with the kitfo." He said with a nod, but kept his eyes on the road.

"Just so you know, I'll be asking questions whenever I see a new kind of house," he laughed but his focus stayed on the road. I missed his eyes on me, which of course was just…not good.

"I'll be happy to tell you if I can. My family is from the Amhara tribe in the north, so I don't know all the types of houses down here. But we can ask the guys. They'll know." He smiled and spoke in Amharic to the guys in the back, who uttered a barrage of *eshis* and nods at whatever Elias told them.

After a moment we quieted down, and I discreetly ran my eyes over Elias. He was wearing his Ray-Ban aviators—which looked so fucking hot on him—and an Aid USA hoodie. His curls held back with the ever-present elastic band. His lips were a dark brown, slightly darker than his skin, and they were perfect. The thought of sucking that bottom lip into my mouth and making him moan as I nibbled on it had me squirming in my seat.

Thankfully Elias saved me from myself and spoke up. "I think we're okay to put it on. We should be on this road for the next hour or so."

"Oh, okay," I said reluctantly. Suddenly, playing this audiobook felt like a life-or-death situation, but I just hit play and sat back.

It was what it was. If Elias turned out to be a homophobe, I'd ask to be on another team and that'd be the end of it.

CHAPTER 5

There was nothing to worry about.

From the first words, the story and the narration by Lin-Manuel Miranda enthralled us both. Every so often we would both grunt in approval or sympathy with Ari, the narrator, who was in the throes of discovering who he was. Growing into who he would be, and falling in love with his best friend. We were on our fourth day in the field, and as Elias started the truck and got on the road headed to lunch, he spoke while looking straight ahead. "Can we keep listening to Ari and Dante?"

We were about two-thirds into the book and I suspected that very soon Dante, Ari's best friend, was going to tell him how he felt. My own coming out had been bittersweet. I'd decided to tell my parents after my dad came back from that last trip, which he never returned from. At that point it was more like the rainbow-colored elephant in the room, and I'd been sure my parents would be fine with it. It was just a matter of finally saying it out loud, making it real. But when my dad died, it became one more thing that would never be whole because he wasn't there.

Elias cleared his throat, and I realized I'd never responded to his request.

"Sorry. I'll start it. We only have like, two hours left, actually."

"Eshi, we have about thirty minutes to the first site. We can listen until then." There was a certain eagerness to his voice, and I wondered what Elias thought about the book. So far he'd said very little about it, but he listened intently, asking me to pause and repeat certain parts.

Would he be able to empathize with the helpless agony of knowing that saying the truth about yourself could cost you everything? Would he still be the kind and charming man I'd gotten to know in the past week if he knew I was like Ari and Dante?

I looked at him as he listened and tried to figure out the expression on his face. As the story unfolded, and the angst between Ari and Dante grew, Elias would grunt or grip the steering wheel, his brows knitted together. He looked...pained. As I observed his handsome profile, I wondered if Elias understood a lot more than I'd given him credit for.

I stopped the book when he slowed and put on the blinkers, approaching a hotel we'd eaten at a few times already. I turned to him as I reached into my backpack to get my wallet.

"Are we waiting for the others?" I asked, making him glance at the side mirror. His mouth flattened at whatever he saw.

"Looks like Sam's team is behind us. I think Tsehay's is already here."

I could not blame him for his lack of enthusiasm at the prospect of having to sit through another meal with Sam. In the past week, he'd gotten more and more insufferable. He was rude to everyone, and just this morning during a stop at one of the field clinics, he'd gotten in the face of one of our government liaisons. Bonnie's prediction—that he would probably do something to embarrass the entire team—was on point after all.

I sighed wearily as I saw the Cruiser drive into the parking lot behind us, dreading the conversation I needed to have with him about his interaction with the official. "I'm not in the mood for Sam's bullshit today. The way he talked to Mr. Dawit was not okay. That man is in his sixties; I can only imagine how offended he was when Sam all but said he was wasting the nutritional supplements."

45

I was trying to keep my voice neutral. From seeing how people acted around Sam, it was clear just hearing his name was a trigger for some of the team. I turned around to look at Yohannes and Abraham, and they were both glaring at the man in question as he jumped out of the Cruiser in wraparound sunglasses, looking like the very picture of the clueless expat jackass.

I fished my own Wayfarers out of my front shirt pocket and looked at Elias, who was tapping a message on his phone. He still had not said a word about my Sam grievances. When he looked up he seemed sympathetic, but I suspected, like every other time I'd complained about Sam, Elias would take the diplomatic route.

He lifted his gaze from his phone, and after what seemed like a series of deep breaths, he finally spoke. "Tsehay's team has a table for us upstairs," he said with a tight smile. "And as for Sam, it's taken the team here years to build the relationship with the woreda."

I nodded at the word for *district* in Amharic, knowing how hard everyone had worked on that partnership with the government. "I know, I'm sorry. I'll talk to him. I can talk to Mr. Dawit too."

Elias's back went up at that and I knew I'd said the wrong thing. Did he think I'd also been disrespectful to Mr. Dawit?

"I think it's best for Tsehay to talk to Mr. Dawit." His tone was friendly, but final. He must've noticed my reaction because when he spoke again it was softer. "We have to manage those relationships. We should be the ones to go back and make sure everything's okay with the woreda office." He came closer and I caught a whiff of the cologne he used, which smelled like the beach. Here I was thinking Sam was unprofessional while I was seriously considering licking a coworker's neck. "You don't have to worry about fixing this. Tsehay and her team know what to do."

"Fair enough," I conceded, and honestly, as far as dressing-downs went, this was one of the kindest ones I'd gotten.

"Are you going to have the ravioli again?" he asked with humor, clearly done with the conversation.

I decided to let go of my annoyance and take Elias's lead. "Of course I'm getting the ravioli—it's insanely delicious and I can get a gigantic bowl for the equivalent of two dollars."

Elias grinned at my enthusiasm for the pasta dish I ordered every time we ate here. Italy's influence in Ethiopia was well-reflected in their coffee and cuisine. I'd discovered that many restaurants had at least one pasta dish, and so far they had all been winners. This restaurant in particular had delicious homemade spinach ravioli.

As we got to the second-floor terrace of the hotel and spotted our large table in the back, I looked up at Elias. "I won't let you shame me into changing my order, Elias!"

He barked out a laugh, already back to being his sunny self, and my heart started trying to beat right out of my chest.

As we got to the table, Tsehay joined in on the teasing. "Eshi, Desta, your ravioli should be here any minute. As soon as the server saw you getting out of the car, he told the cook to start your food." The rest of the team guffawed at my expense, and I grinned at her ribbing.

"Did he get my drink order too? Because you know I like my half Ambo, half Coca with the ravioli." My mention of the Ethiopian sparkling water mixed with Coca-Cola drink that Elias had introduced me to got them all going again. In just one week, I'd grown so comfortable with everyone—except for Sam, of course. The whole team was open and kind, and so good at what they did. They cared about the program, the children and families we were working with, and despite the arduous nature of the work, Ethiopia so far had been an amazing experience.

This type of project either made people fast friends or made you sick of each other pretty quick. After all, we were usually together almost 24/7 except for sleeping and a few hours here and there. We ate meals together, travelled in the field together, and at the end of the day reconvened for a debriefing and dinner. Typically after a few days I found myself desperate for some alone time, no matter how much I liked the team. But so far I'd been eager for the times with the group. I wasn't going to give a certain logistics coordinator all the credit either. Almost everyone so far had been awesome.

"Do we need to eat at this place again?" Sam's voice got my positive thoughts from the last week on a decidedly different track as I took my seat next to Tsehay.

When I opened my mouth, I took a page from Elias's book, whose entire approach to life seemed to be *kill them with kindness*. "This is the only place for miles and miles that serves non-Ethiopian food, and yesterday you complained about not wanting more injera."

Sam pulled up a chair and slumped into it like the petulant asshole he was, scoffing at my words. "Whatever, man."

He was such a jerk.

I turned my attention to the conversation happening on my right side and proceeded to ignore Sam, who was in the midst of asking his usual thousand questions to the server. Every meal required at least two bouts with an interpreter because he had to ask about every ingredient the food was made with, and had various specifications. I got that sometimes people had food allergies or special diets, but he didn't have to be so fucking rude.

I was blessedly distracted by Tsehay, who brought her head closer to mine to ask a question. "How did it go this morning? Other than the clinic." The *when Sam acted like a jerk and almost got us in trouble with the town officials* was implied.

I nodded as I took a drink from my Ambo/Coca. "It went well. I was impressed by the clinic staff—they are doing really great work with the families. I like that they're doing some counseling with the mothers too."

Tsehay smiled at my comment. "They do a nice job there, and it's our biggest one in the program. They see almost five thousand families a month."

I whistled at the impressive number. It was a huge setup, with nearly a few dozen workers.

Soon we were talking data, and when our food came everyone tucked in, hungry after a long morning in the field. I was so distracted enjoying my delicious lunch that I didn't notice the situation happening at a table on the other side of the terrace—until I saw Elias push his chair back loudly to walk over there.

Tsehay uttered what I suspected was a curse word in Amharic as we both turned our heads, looking to where Sam was seemingly having an argument with two men who had been in the middle of their meal.

"What the fuck?" was all I could say. I leaned to take a closer look as Elias rushed over. When I finally realized who the man was, I groaned, hoping this didn't end up a complete disaster. When I turned my head to look at Tsehay, I saw she was also watching the unfolding scene with a horrified expression.

"Please tell me Sam didn't interrupt Mr. Dawit's lunch to pick a fight," I said, doing my best to keep my voice down.

Tsehay sighed as she got up. I stood as well, deciding they might need reinforcements. There would have to be some damage control, that I was certain of. This man oversaw all the supplements and food delivery the clinics got. It was not a relationship we could afford to lose.

What was Sam thinking?

"Sam, what are you doing?" I was almost proud of myself for managing to get that out without a string of expletives.

Meanwhile, I noticed Elias quietly speaking with the other gentleman at the table as Mr. Dawit sat there, a bite of his lunch still in one of his hands. He looked annoyed and completely put off by Sam's presence.

"What do you mean, what am I doing?" the asshat in question asked me, his hands crossed over his chest. "I was just following up about the clinic. I wanted a straight answer about who oversees the distribution of supplements on the government end."

And he thought interrupting the man while he was eating lunch and yelling at him in a crowded restaurant was the way to do that?

I looked over at Elias and Tsehay, who were now tag teaming the table, and got closer to Sam, figuring I'd heed Elias's words and deal with the American while they cleaned up the mess Sam had made. "This is not how you approach these things. You've been doing this work long enough to know that being aggressive and overly direct is not the way to go. You're being rude," I said as quietly as I could. I was pretty sure both of the men at the table spoke English.

Thankfully, something of what I said must have landed, because Sam moved away from the table and stood with me to the side. I smiled and lifted a hand to the men at the table, and gestured for Sam to follow me to where our team was witnessing the whole sordid scene.

When we finally sat down, it seemed Sam had realized that he'd completely mishandled the situation. "I just need this guy to tell me when he's going talk to us."

"Now is not the time," I bit off, still watching Elias and Tsehay, who were now bumping shoulders with the officials and nodding at whatever they were being told. After a moment they walked off, heading back to our table, leaving the two men to their now almost certainly cold lunch.

Sam looked like he was about to argue some more when Elias and Tsehay came back to the table. As they sat down, I leaned over to Elias and said, "Thanks for helping with that."

He gave me a tight smile and turned to Sam. "He said we can come to the office next week." He cleared his throat, as if unsure how to deliver the next part of the update. He didn't shy away from Sam, though—he looked at him straight in the eyes when he spoke. "He asked that either Tsehay or Desta attend the meeting, though."

Sam immediately got red in the face, his expression turning cold. "Who told you to get involved in this?"

I sucked in a breath at the callousness in Sam's tone. His words clearly implied that Elias, being a lowly logistics coordinator, had no business talking on our behalf. Even though so far this week, Elias had made sure things ran smoothly in every way possible. Not to mention that if he had not intervened just now, there probably wouldn't have been any chance at an interview with anyone.

I was about to say something, but once again Elias stood his ground. "I got involved when I saw there might be an issue with the way we were communicating. Mr. Dawit has been working with Aid

USA for a long time. I know him from other program visits. Personal relationships are important here."

Sam had a nasty grin on his face when he spoke again, his eyes intentionally trained away from Elias. "Next time I'm trying to do my work, I'd appreciate if the support staff would keep to their jobs."

The tension at the table was palpable, and it was harder and harder to not yell at Sam. I almost did, but when I opened my mouth to do so, Elias caught my eye and shook his head. His gaze was weary but surprisingly unaffected, like Sam's vitriol was more tiring than anything else. I wondered how many times he'd had to deal with people like Sam. Despite the urge to rail at Sam for his stupidity, I acquiesced to Elias's request and quietly went back to my lunch as everyone else did the same.

When I was done, I looked over at Elias and saw he was limply holding a piece of food in his eating hand as he stared at something in the distance. Of course these things affected him. Of course he felt frustrated. He just couldn't show it. He had to swallow the words I was sure were trying to crawl out of his throat. Because if he got into something with Sam, he most likely wouldn't win.

* * *

THE REST of the afternoon was blessedly uneventful. After the awkwardness of lunch, everyone split off to go do the second part of the village visits, and by the time we got back to the hotel, dusty and exhausted, we all seemed to have shaken off the worst of the day.

As Elias pulled into the hotel, I heard his phone chime a few times with the sound that I recognized as his text messages notifications. I heard Yohannes and Abraham's phones do the same. Mine was buried somewhere in my bag, so if it was a message from the Addis office, I'd just hear it from them.

It was Friday night and most of us had decided to stay in the field for the weekend instead of doing the five-hour drive to Addis and returning Sunday evening. I was running through the list of shows I'd downloaded on my computer, considering which one to watch after dinner, when Elias called my name. And like it happened whenever I heard the word coming from his lips, my chest lurched.

"What's up?"

He was grinning and going between typing a message and looking at me. "Tsehay is organizing an outing. There's a new place that has traditional dancing in town, and she was wondering if you wanted to come."

I perked up at that, my Netflix downloads instantly forgotten. It'd been a long week and relaxing with a beer or two sounded amazing. "Sure, I'm in." Then I thought better of it and wondered if Sam would get an invite too. I was not in the mood for his bullshit, though a chance to be with Elias for the evening was pretty damn appealing.

I must've been pulling a face, because a moment later I heard a small laugh coming from Elias's side. "It's just a few of the Habesha staff coming, and you."

My mother always told me I would never win at poker. My feelings had a tendency to show up right on my face. So I was sure I was sporting a ridiculous grin when I nodded in answer to Elias. "I'm definitely down. What time?"

Elias looked back at the guys, who were about to jump out, and asked a question before turning to me. "There's dinner there too, so maybe an hour?"

"See you then," I said with a smile, and he answered with one just as radiant.

Oh Desta Joy, you are playing with fire, and you don't even care.

CHAPTER 6

I walked into the lobby of the hotel in my usual jeans and long-sleeve T-shirt ensemble, since I had not really planned for an evening outing while I was here. At least I was wearing leather Chucks instead of muddy hiking boots. I wasn't sure what type of dress code we'd have, but I figured that they'd give the farenji a pass for showing up underdressed. I looked around but didn't see anyone from the group. I was glancing at my watch, wondering if I was late, when I felt a tap on my shoulder.

"Hey." Elias smelled like bay rum and the beach, as he always did, and I actually had to restrain myself from leaning in to sniff him.

"Hey yourself. Are we the first ones down?"

He shook his head and pointed in the direction of the hotel entrance doors. "Tsehay's out there getting a taxi. We didn't want to use the Aid vehicles since we're not going to be working tonight. Shall we?"

The question was delivered with a wave of his hand and a very mischievous smile. And he looked *so* good. Also in jeans, but on his feet he had his black Birkens. I'd noticed those were his evening footwear of choice here in Awassa, where the nights were definitely warmer than in Addis. His shirt was a traditional Ethiopian tunic—white with black, red, green, and yellow embroidery on the collar, hem, and sleeves. Like always, his curls sprung in every direction. It was hard to focus with him this close, but somewhere in the recesses of my mind I knew he was probably waiting for a response that wasn't a moan or me pawing at his chest.

"Sure, let's go."

I swallowed hard as he smiled at me, leading the way outside. Sometimes I felt like Elias had to think I was a weirdo, because every once in a while I'd catch him giving me a look that was somewhere between curiosity and something very close to bewilderment. Like he was still not sure what I was, but he was getting a kick out of finding out. That was as far as I went on that particular mental exercise, because nothing good was going to come from me deciding Elias saw me as anything more than an expat who was mostly okay to deal with.

Once outside we joined Tsehay, and I looked around our small group. "It's just us?"

Tsehay rolled her eyes as Elias negotiated a fare with one of the taxi drivers at the hotel. "Some of the staff have family who live in towns close by and went to stay with them for the weekend, and the others said they're too tired." She grinned at me. "So you're stuck with us. Are you ready to do the Eskista?" she asked as she popped her shoulders back and forth.

Elias turned around in that moment and laughed as he gestured for us to get in the car. "Leave him alone, Tsehay. He might not want to do traditional dances."

Despite my mother being Dominican, I wasn't the most avid of dancers, but as per usual the desire to impress Elias had me wanting to act a fool. Once inside the taxi, I said to Tsehay, who was still trying to bop her head from side to side despite the cramped backseat, "I'm up for learning. But I'm not sure I can move my shoulders or my neck like that."

Elias turned around and grinned at us. "We'll teach you, Desta. You have your name to live up to, after all."

My stomach clenched every time Elias looked at me like he and I were in on the same joke. It felt intimate in a way that freaked me out a little bit. Every minute I spent with him had me throbbing with a want I knew very well I could never ever act on.

We got to the place and were seated at a tall, round table, which was surrounded by low wooden stools. I glanced around, taking in the scene. The place looked more like a big event hall than the bar I expected, and there were a lot of people there already.

A server came by soon after we sat down to ask if we needed anything. Elias looked over to me and asked very seriously, "Would you join us in a coffee ceremony?"

I was already pushing it with the amount of coffee I'd had that day, but we had off tomorrow and I was not turning down anything Elias offered me at this point. "Sure," I said with more perkiness than warranted.

Once we'd placed our orders, we turned our attention to the big stage and the performers who were dancing in the style of one of the Ethiopian tribes. I leaned over to ask which one it was and noticed that Elias and Tsehay were talking with their heads close together. They were sitting right next to me but were speaking in Amharic, and I had no hope of understanding a word they were saying.

I almost interrupted them when I saw the ghost of a smile on Elias's lips at whatever Tsehay was telling him. It looked intimate. From out of nowhere, a flare of jealousy burned in my gut. I wanted to be the one sharing a secret with Elias, the only person to put that smile on his face. I wondered if there was something between the two of them. And the flare turned into a full-fledged fire.

Was I chaperoning a date?

A tap on my shoulder pulled me out of the hot mess going on in my head.

"The bunna's here." Elias's smile was cautious, like he could tell something was bothering me.

I tried to smile back as I turned to look at our server, who was busy setting up, and tried to focus on the many things she was doing to get our drinks ready.

Coffee ceremony in Ethiopia was not in any way figurative. It was a communal and drawn out event, performed with great care. It was all done at tableside, and it had all the trappings of a ritual.

After observing for a moment, I sank into the warmth of Elias's body as he leaned in closer to explain, "She's going to roast the raw beans for us."

I was very proud of myself for not shivering when his breath fluttered against my ear. His closeness making me forget my moment of jealousy.

Once I'd gotten it together and was mostly sure a moan wouldn't come out of my mouth, I pointed at the clay pot that looked like a giant version of one of those oil and vinegar bottles. In the most controlled voice I could manage I asked Elias, "What's this called? My mom has a few of them at home, but I forgot the name.

Again he looked delighted at my awareness of all things Ethiopian. "It's a gebena. She'll set it on the coals to brew and we will have bunna in a few minutes."

The roasting beans already smelled delicious and I inhaled deeply. "This is great. It was on my list of things to do."

He dipped his head and pointed to the corn kernels our server was pouring out. "It comes with popcorn."

I nodded in appreciation. "As if the coffee wasn't already perfect on its own, you guys had to make it next-level by adding a delicious snack."

He let out one of those startled laughs that happened when I was being particularly farenji-like. "You are very easy to please when it comes to coffee."

I moaned when I got another strong whiff of the roasting beans. "This place is going to ruin me. Coffee will never be the same again."

Tsehay, who had been doing something on her phone, popped back into the conversation at my coffee addiction confession. "I'm sorry, but it is true. You have tasted the best now, so everything else will pale in comparison."

For some reason, I stared at Elias while she said that, and my thoughts veered to tasting something decidedly not coffee-related.

Get it together, Desta Joy.

"So," I said, desperate for a distraction. "That was a really awkward situation at lunch."

Tsehay and Elias shared another look that once again made me wonder if there was more to their relationship. Tsehay was the one to answer, though. "Sam's been on other projects. We're used to him being…abrupt."

I smiled at her valiant effort at diplomacy. "He was a jackass, and thankfully you guys were there to intervene."

They both looked down, clearly refraining from expressing an opinion. I'd been around enough to know how these things went. Sometimes being candid with the expats could backfire spectacularly, and Elias and Tsehay didn't know me well enough to trust I wouldn't end up telling on them to their boss. After a few more seconds of awkward silence, Elias looked at me, and I could tell he was trying to read what my silence meant, like he was warring with the impulse to trust me.

He exhaled before he spoke, but he seemed determined to say exactly what was on his mind. He ran a hand over his chin, thoughtful as always. "There are people who come to our country and they've already made up their mind that they know better than us." He twisted his mouth in an expression of distaste, and I could see the same fire there as when he'd spoken to Sam earlier. This was not a man to let people walk all over him. He knew his place in the world, even if assholes like Sam could never wise up to it. "Some people can't be reasoned with. Sam thinks that because he does work in this part of the world, that somehow shields him from having to be a decent person. To see us like his equals."

He lifted a shoulder then, as if he were too tired to care. "He's not the first, won't be the last."

Tsehay shook her head, and when she spoke her voice was low, careful. "The problem with Sam is that he can be vindictive if he feels like he's been slighted." She looked at Elias, her expression serious, but she didn't say more as they exchanged looks.

I was still puzzled about their relationship, but decided that whatever it was, I needed to calm the fuck down.

"I just want you both to know that this stays between us. I would never mention this to anyone," I said, while I waited for my coffee to cool. I regretted having brought this up at all. I was ruining the mood, but both Tsehay and Elias seemed to relax.

After a moment of drinking our coffee in a semi-tense silence, Tsehay smiled and moved closer to me. "So did you have a special someone back home? Do you want help picking out some gifts?"

Her tone was casual and friendly, but still I straightened my back and tried to figure out from her expression if there was a hidden agenda behind that question. Did she have suspicions about me? Did she notice anything with me and Elias?

I glanced at him sitting on the other side of Tsehay, and his expression was completely blank. Nothing to show me if he'd heard what she said. The only thing giving him away was the way he was tapping the side of the small cup. A little nervous gesture that tempted me to find out what would happen if I actually told the truth.

I turned to Tsehay again, sure by now that she'd figured out I didn't have a good answer to her question. It wasn't like I hadn't been asked this before. I was well into my marrying years in most of the countries I worked in, so getting asked about my wife or kids happened on pretty much every work trip. I usually answered with something vague or said I was too busy with work for romance, but this time I just didn't feel like doing that.

I put my coffee cup back on the small table and turned so that I was looking right at Tsehay. "Nope." I counted, one, two, three breaths, my heart doing its best to beat right out of my chest, and just said it. "I had a boyfriend, but we broke up before coming on this trip."

Elias's cup rattled as he put it back, making me jump, but his face was not unkind. More like he was flustered by the answer.

Tsehay, on the other hand, squeezed my forearm hard and winked at me. "You don't want to tell anyone else that." She waved a finger between Elias and herself. "And we won't, either."

I nodded, but didn't know what else to say, and it seemed it wasn't necessary. From then on I just focused on the dancers as Tsehay and Elias offered explanations about the different tribal styles and dress. It was all so fascinating I almost—but not quite—missed the long looks Elias sent my way after my big revelation.

CHAPTER 7

The rest of the weekend went on without a hitch. Saturday we went swimming at one of the lakes, and Sunday I spent most of the day sleeping and telling myself all the reasons why going to look for Elias was a terrible, no good, dangerous idea.

But by Monday morning I was itching to see him. I should've anticipated that Sam was going to serve us with some bullshit first thing.

I was making my way through the restaurant, heading for breakfast, when I saw Tsehay and Sam in a heated discussion. There was obviously something wrong because Sam was red in the face and kept swinging his hands as he talked. I braced myself for whatever foolery this was. Knowing Sam and the way he ran his mouth, I anticipated having our whole day turned upside down by whatever he had done.

I got to them just as Elias was coming in from the side door of the restaurant that led to the parking lot. He'd probably been preparing the supplies for the day out, but I had a feeling his meticulous schedule was about to get disrupted.

"What do you mean I can't go out today?" Sam's voice boomed throughout the restaurant, making the diners at the other tables turn their heads in our direction.

"Sam, get it together," I warned through gritted teeth as I literally raised a hand to push him back. "Give Tsehay some room." He'd been crowding her like the asshole he was, but he moved, looking startled when he realized how close he was to her.

I was about to start asking what the hell was going on, but Elias beat me to it and his tone sounded as strained as mine. "What happened?" He was looking at Tsehay, and I suspected it was because if he paid too much attention to Sam, like me, he'd be tempted to pop him on the mouth.

Tsehay looked angry, an expression that didn't seem to go with her usual easygoing personality. I could tell she was trying to come up with an explanation, and the fact that Sam's lips were currently sealed told me he was responsible for whatever had caused the argument.

She sighed and turned to look at me. "Mr. Dawit has requested a different team leader for his woreda."

"What did you do?" I growled as the oaf in question reddened.

Sam tried to posture, but something in my face must have told him I was not in the mood, and clearly neither were Elias or Tsehay. "I ran into him yesterday and asked him some questions, and I guess he didn't like my tone."

I dug my fingers into my eyes as I heard matching groans coming from the others. "So you cornered a government official on his day off to ask him questions after we'd already told you to let us handle the communication with him?" I was barely keeping my patience in check.

"I don't get what the big deal is."

I was about to explain, but Elias jumped in, looking like he was done holding his tongue with Sam. "The big deal is that you've already disrespected Mr. Dawit." His tone was placid enough, and his voice was not a decibel above proper inside voice, but no one could not mistake the edge in it. "If you cannot mind the social rules and the ways that our people conduct themselves when working with offi- cials, then you are going to impact this project's development."

This man was very close to losing his patience. My whole body woke up and took notice because take-charge Elias was hot as fuck.

Sam's face went from flushed to mottled with an angry red, and I could almost hear the gears in his idiotic head turning. He opened his mouth, but before he did something that he could never take back, I intervened. "There is nothing to say, Sam. You fucked up and now you have to sit this one out."

He balked at that, but I wasn't standing by and letting Sam sabotage this entire project because he couldn't keep his fool mouth shut. I ignored him and turned again to Tsehay and Elias. "How far behind will we get if we only send out two teams this week?" Another yelp came from Sam's direction, but I didn't bother looking his way as I waited for an answer.

"It will throw off the schedule completely," Tsehay answered, and the furrow in her brow told me I didn't need to point out that kind of setback would be catastrophic for our already-tight deadline.

Elias nodded, already tapping something on his tablet. "We timed it so we'd be done here and at the new sites just as they were gearing up for their quarterly health checks with the families. We can't get delayed."

"That's right. Dammit," I said, this time turning to glare at Sam. "You need to figure out how to make amends with Mr. Davit so you can get back to work. For now we need to stay on task. What do you suggest, Elias?"

He gave me a funny look like he didn't expect me to ask him what to do, but as far as I could tell, he and Tsehay were the ones that knew what we needed to do to stay on our timeline.

Tsehay spoke while he mulled the question over. "Eli can lead Sam's team."

Before the man in question could even contemplate complaining, I shut him up. "Don't." I wasn't even sure what I was objecting to, but at least Sam knew enough not to piss me off again.

"What do you think?" I asked Elias as he considered Tsehay's suggestion. I was extremely aware of the fact that even though I knew this was probably the best solution, I was dreading not having Elias with me all day. That I'd been looking forward to listening the rest of *Aristotle and Dante* with him.

"I can do that." He dipped his head at my question, but something in his eyes made me wonder if he was bummed out too. I reminded myself that the only dummy in this equation was me, and Elias was probably more concerned about us being able to do our job.

He looked at Sam, who was still fuming next to us, and clenched his jaw hard. "We can switch one of Sam's workers with Yohannes, who has the nutrition background, since that's something I'm not familiar with."

Sam scoffed like an asshole and I glared in his direction. Elias looked like he was ready give the man a piece of his mind. "You have to go and apologize to Mr. Dawit. He is a reasonable man, but you have publicly disrespected him. Tsehay and I were going to talk to him, but you made this mess. So you will have to fix it."

"What?" He had the gall to sound offended. "All I did was ask a couple of questions."

This time Elias straightened to his full height, and I could see why he always kept that easy and quick smile. He didn't need to assert himself with posturing. This man was perfectly capable of owning a room when he wanted to.

"Sam, does your mother work?"

The question seemed to catch him off guard, and he actually stammered. "Yes, my mother works," he said haughtily. "She's a high school principal."

Elias smiled, but his eyes were still very unfriendly. "How would you feel if people came up to your mother at restaurants and on her way home from church on Sunday to tell her she doesn't know how to do her job?"

Tsehay made a sound that I was pretty sure was a suppressed laugh, and I had to bite my tongue not to chuckle. Sam spluttered, furious for getting called on his bullshit. "That's not—"

I cut him off because no one had time for this. "The hell it isn't. What you did was disrespectful and Mr. Dawit has a right to an apology," I told him, already walking away. Sam could get as red in the face as he wanted. That had to be said.

Tsehay and Elias took their cues from me, and we all hurried out to where the teams were waiting by the vehicles. "I think this is a good plan," I said as we got outside. "But let's make sure we have a long debrief tonight."

As everyone rushed off, I stood rooted to the passenger side of my vehicle. I realized that even though I was ready for the work, there was pang of loss in my chest that I would spend the day without Elias. Like he could read my mind, his voice called from somewhere behind me.

"Desta." I tipped my head up to look at him, trying very hard to keep inside the things that wanted to come out of my mouth. "Don't listen to Ari and Dante without me."

My gut turned liquid at the conspiratorial humor in this voice. "Okay."

He winked at me, and my extremities went numb while all the blood rushed up to my head. "I'll see you tonight."

I was sure that had only sounded like a promise to me, but still I watched him go. His long limbs eating up the gravel as he went to his vehicle, that gorgeous ass encased in dark blue jeans. He always wore his work shirts tucked in, making him look neat and trim and edible. He was a beautiful man and he seemed so completely unaware of it, which just made my thirst for him that much more pronounced.

"Are you really going to let them do this?"

Fucking Sam.

I sighed as I peeled my eyes off Elias's powerful forearms pulling on the door of the Cruiser and turned my attention on Sam. "They didn't do anything. *You did.* I suggest you apologize before you ruin the entire week for the team."

I didn't bother waiting for an answer and got into the truck, which already had Sam's usual driver sitting at the driver's seat since Elias would be driving for that team.

Our tiny convoy drove out of the gravel parking lot for the day in the field. I kept my eye on Elias's truck until our own vehicle took a turn in the opposite direction. And when my eyes drifted to the clock on the dashboard, I barely managed to keep myself from counting the hours until I'd see him.

CHAPTER 8

I made myself go up to my room first.

The day had its low moments, but it had been mostly good. My team, despite the last-minute changes, got the work done, and from the texts I'd gotten from Tsehay and Elias, it seemed like they also did fine. Not that I expected any different. Figured that Sam being out of the picture would make no difference.

Except there had been one difference.

I'd missed Elias.

Throughout the day I'd constantly found myself turning to ask him about something I saw on the road or about the book I was reading. I'd missed his presence literally, his body next to me in the Land Cruiser. And the little things, like the way his eyebrows popped over the top of his sunglasses when I said something to make him laugh.

I'd been doing that—collecting comments and things I thought he'd find funny. I liked seeing Elias smile. It's not like he was stingy with them either; his face was open and bright for everyone. And people were drawn to him because of it. But there was one kind of smile that tugged at one side of his mouth and made the corners of his eyes crinkle. That one only happened when I was being a particular brand of smart-ass, which my fool head decided made it *my* smile. And I was hopelessly addicted to it. I'd been desperate to see it all day.

I made it upstairs without interacting with anyone and rushed through getting ready for dinner. I tossed my dusty clothes in a corner and jumped in the shower, not even bothering to turn on the water heater, making quick work of getting clean and dressed. In less than ten minutes I was walking downstairs again, my laptop over my shoulder.

At one point during the day we'd made plans to have a working dinner in a small private room next to the restaurant, which Elias had reserved. He'd said that way our group would be able to debrief without bothering the other diners. Because he thought of everything. I pressed a hand to my chest as I made my way to the room, my stupid heart already skipping in anticipation of seeing him. It was sad how far gone I was. It hadn't even been twelve hours since I'd been with the man, and here I was acting like a lovesick teenager.

I stepped in and found him alone in the room, and I took a second to look at him. A smarter person would have made note of the way my entire body ran hot just from seeing him and kept their distance, but I couldn't bother with being rational at the moment. I moved to slide my water bottle into my bag, and the sloshing sound made him pop his head up. When he saw me he smiled wide, like I was the best thing he'd seen all day. And all I wanted to know was: how was I supposed to rein myself in when he looked at me like that?

"Hey," I said, lifting a hand up like a complete jackass.

"Desta." He gestured toward the seat next to his on the table. "Sit. Tsehay's team only got in like ten minutes ago, so they're running behind."

I waved a hand at that. Tsehay's team had the farthest to go today, so it made sense for her to need more time. And she would probably not forgo a hot shower because she was rushing to catch Elias alone like I had. "Oh, I'm fine to wait. That'll give me time to check my email."

He gave me an assessing look, as if he were making sure that no body parts had gone missing in his absence. Or maybe that was just what I wished he were thinking. "You had time to shower."

I dipped my head and stared freely, since he was doing the same to me. He looked freshly showered too. He had on a gray sweatshirt and tan linen pants, and as usual in the evenings, his Birkens. "I was glad to get back to the hotel today." I refrained from blurting out that was mostly due to my thirst for him.

"Did anything happen?" he asked, all commanding. Like he was ready and able to deal with whatever it was. A shiver ran down my spine, but this one took the route that went straight to my dick.

"Nothing bad happened," I reassured him as I got my laptop plugged in. "Although I may have to take a hiatus from coffee."

I was making a show of arranging my stuff on the table, but kept an eye on him to get his reaction. He actually jumped in surprise at my words, and his puzzled expression almost made me laugh. "No bunna? Something must have happened."

You would've thought I'd said that I going to start working buck naked, but I still felt all warm and fuzzy at how seriously he took my caffeine obsession.

I shifted so I could face him, ready to fill him in. "Well, in part I blame you," I said, barely able to keep from grinning.

He read my expression, and I saw when he realized that this was going to be one of our jokes. He could do that, just tune into my moods. I thought about how Miguel never quite got my humor. I'd come home with a funny story from work or my commute, and he'd stare at me blankly until the smile died on my face. I'd told myself again and again that maybe it was lost in cultural translation. And yet with Elias, from the first day we'd found a million things in common to laugh, talk, or even rant about. Even after just one week it felt completely natural.

"How could I be blamed for your coffee hiatus? I mostly drink tea," he said in feigned disgruntlement.

"It would've been nice to be warned that I could get ghee and salt in my bunna. I almost threw up in one of the families' houses, Elias," I lamented with my hands over my face, actually remembering the embarrassment. "It wasn't even that it tasted bad, it was just so unexpected."

I could hear that he was making an effort not to laugh, wheezing and rumbling coming from beside me. When I took my hands off my face, I found him grinning while he shook his head, clearly biting his tongue.

"Don't laugh at me, Elias. I threw up in my mouth!" Keeping a straight face was out of the question at this point. It was just a matter of who burst out laughing first.

He clicked his tongue, obviously not wanting to be the one to break, but he was showing more teeth by the second. "Desta, I can't leave you even for one day." He was kidding, of course, playing along with the game I started, but his words pummeled me.

"I'm hopeless," I conceded, when what I'd wanted to say was, *I missed you. I felt your absence all day.*

He must've seen something in my face, because the humor in his eyes changed to something more subdued, but in no way less warm. "You're not hopeless." The way he said it, low and earnest, like he needed me to believe it, was almost too much. The air around us shifted and I leaned toward him. For what, I wasn't sure. I just needed to be closer.

I could see his throat working, like he was struggling with making words too. I opened my mouth to say something that could bring back the humor from before. But at that same moment the door to the room burst open and two servers arrived with the drinks and snacks I assumed Elias had pre-ordered.

I shook my head as they moved around, trying to get myself together, and Elias stood up so fast his phone bounced off the table. He dove to catch it and knocked over his chair, making the servers stop what they were doing to look in our direction. Elias told them something in Amharic that sounded self-deprecating, or maybe that was just me projecting. But he had lost his footing for a second there. Elias, who was always the very picture of cool, calm, and collected, had gotten flustered. I wasn't enough of a fool to think that it was because he'd been affected by me, but I did need to remember to keep my boundaries in check.

* * *

THERE WERE no more awkward moments or inside jokes after that. A few minutes after our food arrived, the rest of the team started trickling in, and soon we were caught up in our work. Even Sam had been on his best behavior, at one point thanking us for making sure we didn't get behind in the surveys. Tsehay had discreetly let me know Mr. Dawit had called Bonnie in Addis, so I figured she'd given him the riot act.

But now it was almost past ten and everyone had gone to bed except for Elias and me. I wasn't lying to myself—I was here because I was greedy for some time alone with him. We'd have another two days working in separate teams, and I had no self-control, so here we were. Elias, who had been putting away his laptop while making notes on his iPad, looked down at my stuff, which was still sprawled over the table.

"Do you have more to do?" He knew I didn't, since I'd said as much to Tsehay before she left, but I went along with whatever kept us talking.

"Not really, just giving myself a moment to breathe before heading up." I stretched my arms over my head, getting the kinks out of my tired muscles. Elias kept his eyes on my face as I did it.

I could feel that he had something he wanted to say, and my stomach flipped, wondering if I'd made him uncomfortable before. But if I had, why would he still be here with me?

No, maybe he just wanted to make sure we left the room like we'd found it. That was it. He'd reserved it and didn't want people leaving a mess.

"Are you heading to bed?" I asked, my mouth overriding the lecture about boundaries I'd given myself just a few hours ago.

He looked at me for another minute, and again I felt that charged but comfortable silence from earlier. I usually hated long silences—as an only child I'd had to endure them constantly, especially after my dad died—and I always felt compelled to fill them. But with Elias, I didn't. It was like I could let my mind drift, and even if it went to a place I didn't like, I wouldn't get stuck in there.

"I'm heading up soon," he said, then raised his chin in the direction of my laptop. "I'll wait for you to pack up."

He stopped and looked at me again like he was deciding whether or not to say what was on his mind. I turned my attention to clearing my things off the table while he weighed whatever he was considering. Telling myself that if he really had been weirded out, he wouldn't have stayed behind in this room with me.

Finally, he spoke. "Desta."

I looked up at him, somewhere between wary and hopeful. "Yeah?"

"Would you like to go for a walk in the garden?" He paused and then added, "With me."

I stood up faster and more eagerly than what was probably prudent, and slung my bag over my shoulder as a grin cut across my face. This was a friendly gesture, I told myself. He was just being polite, but I couldn't stop the racing in my heart when I answered.

"I'd love to."

CHAPTER 9

The first three weeks of the survey flew by, and after travelling for days on end all over southern Ethiopia, I was more than a little in love.

Like my parents, I'd been completely charmed by this country's boundless beauty. My eyes couldn't get enough of the sprawling coffee fields and mountain ranges. The people, especially, had been amazing. Ethiopians were brimming with humor and hospitality. Every village we stopped in, people were always smiling or wanting to practice their English with me.

But the best parts were the times with Elias. Despite my attempts to keep a professional distance, I'd gotten more and more pulled in by him. Every single thing I learned about the man made me want him more. After that night when we'd ended up working together and took a walk in the garden, something had changed with us. Even when we were on different teams—and we'd had to be a few times until Sam made amends with Mr. Dawit—we'd reconnect in the evenings. Sometimes it could be a quick catch-up to plan what new book we'd listen to—Ari and Dante had been the first of many. At times we went on a stroll before bed, but it seemed like my days in Ethiopia were not complete without Elias.

We'd been together almost every day of the trip, and as we drove up to my guesthouse in Addis, I felt completely unprepared to spend the next few on my own. I didn't even know if he'd be driving me for the next trip south, or if he'd be on one of the other vehicles with a different team. I should've probably been concerned by the level of dread I was feeling about not seeing someone who was essentially a work-related acquaintance. And yet I was too preoccupied with the idea that this could be goodbye to care.

Once we arrived at the guesthouse, Elias killed the ignition, and turned that heart-stopping smile on me. "We made it."

I looked at him and I wondered if it was the ill-advised crush making me see things, but I thought he seemed a little regretful that our trip was coming to an end.

I didn't know how to say goodbye or thank him for how good he'd been to me in the last few weeks, but I was having trouble finding where to start. So I went with rambling. "Thanks so much for everything. I hope you get to relax before going back to work next week. I'm so ready for a shower and some sleep."

He looked like he wanted to say something, but like a moron I opened my mouth before he could. "Okay, so I guess I'll get going."

As I went to open the passenger door, he stopped me. "Do you want to go see some live music tonight? There's a good band that plays on Fridays in town. They do lots of covers and I think you'll love the lead singer."

Oh.

Oh?

Oh!

"Really?" Funny how the tightness in my chest from the last hour loosened instantly. "That sounds great, actually. I told you how much I like live music, and I'd love to see a gig here. I'm in." *Stop talking, Desta, you're now fully in overexcited puppy territory.*

He laughed, shaking his head at my extreme enthusiasm, and I kept going. "If you throw in a dinner with *anything* not containing injera, you'll be my hero. Not that I don't love the stuff, but I'm ready for a pizza or something." I was the first one to admit that my love for injera waned after weeks of eating it cold for at least one meal a day.

"How about pizza and beer? Then music."

I rolled my eyes in ecstasy. "That sounds incredible. What time should I be ready?"

"I'll be here at 7:30. The show doesn't start until 9:00, so we can eat and then walk there. The Beer Garden is right behind the bar where they play."

I gasped at that. "Beer Garden? You really are trying for superhero status."

"Just making sure you get the best of Ethiopia." He grinned in that way that made his dimples pop, and I was a complete fucking goner.

Once he was back in the vehicle, I stood by the entrance to the guesthouse and lifted my hand to him, feeling like this was nowhere near sufficient for a goodbye. "See you in a few hours."

Elias nodded and the intensity in his eyes once again made me wonder what exactly was going through his head. "Eshi, Desta. See you soon."

After I watched him drive away, I climbed the stairs to my room, sporting a grin of my own. Self-recrimination about my poor choices in men flew out the window with every step.

* * *

By 7:15 P.M. I'd changed clothes twice and was doing way too much for what should have just been dinner with a colleague. I'd turned it into a *thing*, and was currently standing in front of the mirror in my room tugging at my dark brown curls, which had become completely unruly in the last few weeks. I'd also gotten a hell of a tan from so many days in the sun. The deeper brown tone of my skin made my hazel eyes look weirdly lighter, like some kind of wild cat. Which, given my current mood, was probably appropriate.

I looked good. Not that it mattered, because this was *not* a date.

Sick of myself and my fretting, I grabbed the black leather bomber jacket I'd brought, and was tugging it on over a green sweater when I heard a knock. I rushed to the door, my heart almost pounding out of my chest. As soon as I opened it, I realized I had not been ready for what was waiting on the other side.

Elias looked fucking edible.

I actually had to lean on the doorframe to keep from coming too close. I tried to discreetly take in what was in front of me, and knew I was failing miserably. He was wearing a white linen shirt under a brown leather blazer, with extremely well-fitting dark blue jeans and red Chucks on his feet. His curls sprung high on his head, held back by his usual thin elastic band. Tonight he was also wearing a few silver bracelets on his wrists, and a wide silver ring on his right hand.

He was such a fine man. His perfectly shaped lips were incredibly distracting, made for kissing, and God, I wanted to.

I realized I'd only opened the door to stare at him, and let out a flustered, "Hi."

The smile he gave me was radiant, like he was so damn glad to see me. I was reading too much into it, I knew that. But when he stared me up and down and kept his eyes on the general area of my mouth for a few seconds longer than warranted, my head, once again, started going places it *shouldn't*.

"Eshi, Desta, are you ready to go?" Maybe I was imagining things, but it sounded to me like he was a little flustered too.

"I am. I took a nap, and now I'm starving."

He grunted in approval, which made my belly flip and the skin on my face tighten. But when he spoke, that's when all the blood in my brain went south all at once. "We have to get you what you need, then."

When we came out of the guesthouse he walked me to an older model Toyota Corolla and held the door open for me. I sent myself another reminder that I was *not on a date* and got into his very well-cared for car. "Wow, this car is *pristine*."

He seemed pleased at my noticing, and by the compliment, but when he spoke he was a little apologetic. "I'm a bit intense about it. Taxes for cars here are really high. And it's almost impossible to get a loan from the bank. It took me a long time to save enough to buy it, so I make sure I care for it."

I smiled at the obvious pride he had in his car and thought of how different things were for us. Even knowing as much as I did about the many inequalities in the world, a lot of them were just that: something I knew about. Not something I'd needed to live with, or through. My work exposed me to them, yes, and I hoped in some way I helped bridge those gaps, but I was always at a safe distance. I didn't really have skin in the game, not like Elias and Tsehay did. Maybe that was why they held themselves to such an impossibly high standard.

"You're a man who knows how to care for things, that's for sure," I said, unable to keep the admiration out of my voice, or my mind from marveling at how he cared for the people in his life.

Elias's smile was the exact reaction I'd been hoping for. "And I employ that care in taking us where we need to go. Are you ready for some beer, pizza, and music, Desta?"

His energy and smile were infectious, and I felt one blooming on my own face as I answered him, "I am so ready."

CHAPTER 10

The "beer garden" turned out to be a microbrewery that made four varieties of delicious German-style beer on site. The owner was an Ethiopian man who'd lived in Bavaria for decades, and had returned home to start his own business.

The place was a trip. Decorated in a mix of German and Ethiopian kitsch, it was packed with people, and there were servers buzzing around in lederhosen, shouting in Amharic and handing off huge steins of homemade beer to customers. The place, the food, and the company had me feeling so content I closed my eyes and sighed deeply after one too many slices of pizza—which apparently was the most popular item in the menu despite not being exactly German.

After a moment, I felt Elias clink my stein with his. I opened my eyes and clinked back, once again pleasantly surprised by how easy it was to be with him.

When I looked at him again, he seemed worried, and after a moment asked me, "Are you too tired? Would you like me to take you back to the hotel?"

The lethargic feeling of the last few minutes evaporated at the thought of losing his company, and I sat up. "No, not at all. I'm excited for the music, but I'm feeling pretty relaxed right now from all the good pizza and beer." I glanced around again, utterly charmed by the place. "This is a great spot. Thanks for bringing me. Addis is full of surprises."

He smiled then, and it looked wistful. "Yes, it is. It's hard for me to think of living anywhere else."

The way he said it made me think he was considering exactly that. "Oh, are you thinking of going abroad?" I asked with way too much interest.

He didn't answer immediately, considering my question as he twisted the wide silver band on his finger. "I've been accepted into a doctoral program at Columbia University, in psychology," he said quietly before taking a long drink.

"Wow," I said, genuinely impressed. "That's great. Congratulations."

After a moment he ran his hand over the tablecloth, smoothing the crease running down the center of table. I could tell he was trying to figure out what to say next. "I was accepted last year, but I deferred." Something about the way he said it made me think the reasons for the deferment hadn't changed much. "I have a few more weeks to decide. If not, I'll lose my spot."

Just the idea of Elias potentially living in the States did unsettling things to me. My chest fluttered, and I could practically feel the blood rushing to my face. Immediately, the possible career change I'd been agonizing over for the last year—and how it could mean a move to New York City—filled my head. A flare of annoyance at myself tamped down some of my inappropriate excitement, and I tried to focus on what Elias said. On how obviously conflicted he was about the decision he needed to make.

I leaned across the table, hoping my smile looked genuine, and not like I was freaking about my own shit like a selfish heel. "That's huge, for real. New York City is a great place to live too. We lived in Upstate New York, about four hours north." I pointed at myself as he listened with interest. "I've never actually lived in the city, but we went a lot when I was growing up, and my friend Lucía is there and loves it."

His eyes widened when I said that, and he kept twisting that ring.

When he finally spoke, he steered away from talking about whatever was conflicting him about going to the States. "I didn't know you were from New York. I thought because your parents did international work you'd be based in DC."

I placed my hand on the table, hyperaware of the fact that if I moved it less than a centimeter, we'd be touching. "Yeah. That's my home base right now, but my mom lives in Ithaca. That's where my dad was from, and we moved there after he died. She wanted to be closer to his family." I shrugged, always feeling awkward when talking about my mom's family. "She was never very close to her own, and they were all in the DR anyways." I played with the slice of half-eaten pizza on my plate, feeling like this whole conversation had suddenly gotten a lot more serious.

"I did college in Ithaca and moved to DC for a job with Aid USA after I graduated. I've been there ever since." I paused, thinking of how little I considered DC as home. "I travel a lot though, so I'm rarely there for more than a few months at a time."

He nodded and looked at me with a focus that made me breathless. Before I knew it, I was putting words to something I hadn't spoken out loud to anyone, not even Lucía.

"I'm actually thinking of leaving DC." I rolled my eyes in self-mockery, trying to give levity to what I was saying, even though I felt every word in the pit of my stomach.

Elias leaned closer as I opened my mouth again, like he understood how big this moment was for me. "Where are you thinking of going?" Elias's questions were always earnest. His focus and attention solely on me.

"I'm thinking of going back to school too. It'll involve a bit of a career shift." I lifted my hand when he raised his eyebrows. "Not a completely new field, but definitely different. I've been considering it for a while. This survey came at the perfect moment, actually. I'm trying to use my time in Ethiopia to decide on what's next."

But instead of doing that, I'm spending an absurd amount of time obsessing about you.

Elias opened his mouth a couple of times, but closed it before he spoke. I could tell he was carefully deciding where to take the conversation. Finally, he said, "This work is not easy. Even when you enjoy it, doing it for too long can be depleting."

I tried to find words to respond, but came up short. Because in reality, I hadn't told myself why I wanted to do something else. I just felt *tired* of where I was now.

"It's partly that, but it's a little bit more selfish, I'm afraid." I shifted in my chair, the conversation making me a little restless. This was never easy for me. I was so much better at listening to people's problems than asking for help about my own.

"The thing is, even though there's a lot about this work I love—and it's definitely meaningful—I'm not sure it's really what I want to do. My dad did this kind of work, and he was great at it. It was his calling, you know? Everyone I've ever met overseas who worked with him always talks about him with such reverence. I just don't know if it's what *I'm* meant to do."

I felt exposed and vulnerable for talking about this. The one huge thing that I'd always known but never wanted to look at so closely.

But when I brought my gaze up to Elias, there was no judgment in his eyes. Then he spoke, and I felt something that I rarely did, even with Lucía. Elias *got* me. "This work is not for everyone. Even for those who love it, after some time, it makes sense to move on."

I breathed in deeply and slowly exhaled before answering, feeling like this conversation was loosening something that had been coiled tightly in my chest for as long as I could remember, sapping my energy without me knowing. "I started out wanting to follow in his footsteps, not just for myself so much, but for my mom. When my dad died, it was like a light went out inside of her, and I was desperate to turn it back on."

I shook my head at the memories of those first few months after my dad died, when we were both like husks walking around our house, obfuscated from grief.

"For a long time, the only moments when she would light up were when she talked about their work and the places they'd been. What they'd done together. I wanted to give some of that back to her, but now I need something different. And it makes me feel like shit because it's an honor to do this work."

My chest tightened again from what I wanted to say next. My sexuality had not come up again since that conversation with Tsehay. Elias finding out I was gay had not changed much between us, and I imagined it was partly because we'd steered clear of it since that day. Even after we finished Aristotle and Dante, he'd just commented on how much he'd liked it without going into much detail. But for some reason, tonight I wanted to push. Hear what he really thought about that part of me. It was stupid and selfish to put him in an awkward position like this, but it seemed vital to know he was okay with that part of me too. "I also struggle with how much of my personal life I have to keep under wraps while I'm overseas."

Elias pulled back then, his back straightening, and I could see his shoulders tense. He opened his mouth once, then closed it again, looking a little panicked. Immediately I felt ashamed of hijacking the conversation and making it about me.

I shook my head and took a big gulp of my beer. "I totally took over this conversation. We were talking about you. It sounds like you're not sure if you want to go. Would you come back after you're finished?"

Elias raised his eyebrows and lifted his hands in a gesture of concession before he answered, "You just said a lot of things I would like to hear more about, but I will let you get away with changing the subject." It was like he could see right through me. "And yes, I am conflicted. I know it's an amazing opportunity, and I would be foolish not to take it, but I'm scared leaving will make it hard for me to come back, and the idea of not returning feels like I'd be betraying my country...and myself."

My impulse was to minimize, say something like *don't put all that on yourself* or *it's your life and you do what you need to*. But then I thought about my own struggle. *I* knew very well that deciding between what made me happy and disappointing those I loved could sometimes feel insurmountable. When I looked at the lines around his mouth, I saw the tension this conversation was bringing up for him.

Elias would get my struggle better than most; his own was very close to mine. That realization made me feel more understood than I had in a very long time. "That's a really big burden to carry."

I sat there, quietly giving him more time to say what was on his mind. After we distracted ourselves with taking sips of beer and attempting to finish the pizza on our plates, Elias finally continued. "I guess it will depend on how I feel once I experience life in a different place. How I take to it, you know? I love Addis, and my family is here, but sometimes I want to have more freedom too."

I cocked my head to the side, not completely certain I understood what he was saying, and was cautious not to make any assumptions. "Do you mean like not living with family?"

He sat very still for a moment, then shook his head. "You know what, it's not important."

I leaned even closer, desperate for him to go on. "No, I want to know. I mean, unless you don't want to tell me your entire life history like I just did to you."

He smiled, and his head came a little closer to mine. It was like our bodies were trying to override the rules by which we were supposed to play. "I like hearing about your life."

His words pulsed through me. Just lit me up, ramping up even more the anticipation of the secret he was about to tell me. It felt like my heart was pounding between my temples. Because I knew what he was about to say, and that both terrified and elated me.

"When I say I want more freedom to be myself, I mean I want to know what it's like to be like you."

The flutter in my chest was intense, like a bird was flapping its wings against my ribcage, and even before I asked the question, I knew the answer. That comment—"like me"—could mean anything, but I knew. I *knew*. I'd known from the first moment.

Still, my voice shook when I asked, "Like me?"

Instantly the energy around us seemed to change. Elias was no longer somber. He was smiling, but he put his hands up. "Okay, now I think I scared you."

Dammit, Elias, *keep talking*. "I'm not scared."

With the smile still on his face, he tapped my foot with his under the table. He leaned in like he wanted to avoid yelling over the noise, but even with chatter all around us his voice was sure and clear. "I'm gay, and I want to know what it's like to live openly. I could never do that here."

All the breath left my body, and not because I had never heard this kind of thing before. I'd been working all over the world for years, at times in places where it was not safe to even discuss LGBTQ rights, much less be openly gay. Hell, I'd dated a few guys who had to live on the DL for their own safety. But Elias's revelation felt like he was opening a door.

I rushed to make sure he knew I understood the kind of trust he was placing in my hands. "Elias, I just want you to know I would never betray your confidence."

He tapped my foot again. "I know, konjo." He gave me the smallest smile, and my entire body buzzed with anticipation.

There was so much more I wanted to say and to ask, but I didn't want to get too intense or seem needy, so I latched onto the only safe thing I could think of to say. "What does that mean? Konjo?"

This time the smile he gave me made my entire body light up. "It means beautiful."

"Oh." I had nothing.

Language escaped me entirely while I sat there, marveling at how the spot on my knee—where it was touching his—throbbed like a beating heart. I frantically searched for a way to respond to Elias's words, as well as the way he was looking at me, but the server brought the check, forcing us to focus on something else for a few minutes.

After arguing about who would pay, we settled on me buying dinner and him paying the cover and drinks at the show. We walked out of the restaurant and headed to the bar, which was in a building across the street. Neither of us mentioned the conversation we'd been having before, or that Elias had come out and basically made it clear he was into me.

I should've been concerned about the fact that I was once again being impulsive, and in a situation that would almost certainly end in

disaster. But these weeks of getting to know him, of starting a friendship, made this all seem like the next logical step. None of it felt
awkward or weird. It felt fine. *I* felt fine.

So I went with it.

The bar was called Black Orchid and it was on the top floor of a
commercial building. When we walked in, we could hear Ethiopian
pop music playing over the speakers. The place was about half full and
it definitely had dark and smoky jazz lounge vibes. The lights were
dim and there were lots of hidden corners. Small candles were placed
at the center of low tables where patrons were lounging on comfort-
able-looking armchairs. The bar was busy, and to the right of it was
the stage, which at the moment had three musicians on it setting up
for the band.

I glanced around, taking in the people in the room. It was a mixed
crowd. There was a wide range of dress too. Some of the women
looking runway ready, while a few of the younger American and
European guys were walking around dressed in what I called "expat
casual." All-weather pants, some sort of high-end sweater/fleece
combo, and hiking boots. I was pretty proud of myself for being one
of the few farenjis actually wearing natural fibers. Because seriously,
who shows up to a clearly nice bar looking like they were going to go
climb Kilimanjaro?

As we walked through the place, Elias ran into some people he
knew and introduced me as his co-worker Desta. As always, every
Ethiopian I met was delighted with my name and wanted to hear the
story behind it. So we stopped and talked with Elias's acquaintances
as we made our way to the bar.

We finally settled in a corner table close to the stage and ordered
some drinks. I was actively trying not to obsess about the fact that I
could probably kiss him. Not here, of course, but if we were somewhere alone, my kiss would be welcome. An image of me pressing my
mouth to his invaded my thoughts. I wondered if he would probably
start by grazing his tongue with mine, tasting me as I did him. Or
maybe he'd just chastely press our lips together.

Elias rapped the table lightly with his knuckles, making me jump right out of my sensual daydream. When I glanced up at him, the grin on his lips told me he had a pretty good idea of what I'd been doing. So yeah, the music needed to start soon, or I was in trouble.

As we waited for the show, I felt compelled to bring up the conversation again. A more prudent person would've talked about something neutral, but not me. I jumped right into the deep and slippery end. "So, have you dated? Are you dating someone now? I would stop, but you opened that can of worms, and now I want to know everything."

He laughed and sipped the sparkling water he'd ordered. "I've dated. I can't say it's gone well, but I've tried." His face didn't look like it'd been good at all. I thought he would leave it at that, but he continued. "About six months ago I ended a relationship with someone after about a year. He worked for the British Embassy. In the consular office."

He stopped there and looked at the stage, but tonight I was apparently letting my pushiness do whatever it wanted, so I prodded for more. "Why did you break it off? Did he go home?"

His face turned ashen then, and I almost regretted asking. Still I didn't change to topic, because I wanted to know. "He didn't. He had about one more year left here when we ended things, but he left early, asked for a transfer. He never really liked Addis." He raised a shoulder, trying to feign an indifference I could see was not really there. "This was his first posting in Africa, and I think he would've preferred something in Asia or Europe. Somewhere less 'rough,' as he liked to say."

His face was a mix of sadness and mortification, and I felt so pissed on his behalf. The guy must've been one of those who went into the Foreign Service expecting to jump from European countries to "exotic" locations, only socializing with other expats. God forbid they had to interact with the people who lived in the countries. Unless, of course, they wanted to use them as part of the entertainment.

"What happened then? Did he cheat on you?" I asked, already pissed off for him.

Elias shook his head, a rueful smile on his lips. "Americans, you're always so direct. To be honest, I don't know if he cheated," he said, again trying hard to seem unaffected. But I could see in his knitted brows and the lines around his mouth that it still bothered him. "I wouldn't be surprised if he did. Byron was very adventurous in bed and he was always teasing me about being too conservative. I wasn't interested in sleeping with anyone other than him, and that made me a 'victim of my country's antiquated moralistic beliefs.'"

I felt like shit for pushing him, and almost told him he didn't need to explain, but before I did, he spoke again. "I overheard him talking to one of his colleagues about me, and what he said was not something a person who cared for me would say." He shook his head and looked so embarrassed. "When I confronted him, he tried to convince me I heard things out of context, but it wasn't first time he'd been disrespectful. I think the hardest part for me was that I trusted him."

I wanted to hold his hand, comfort him as he spoke of things that were clearly still painful, but I couldn't. Not out here in the open. I touched his knee under the table instead, which was not nearly enough, but already much more than I could probably get away with. "That's so fucked up, Elias. I'm sorry."

His expression was one of resignation. "I opened up to him about painful and personal things, and he turned around and used those same things to talk to me like I was some kind of simpleton."

He smiled and touched my hand, which was still on his knee. "Byron's not the first man I've been with, but he was the first person I trusted enough to talk about some of my struggles. It's not easy being a gay man in Ethiopia. So many times I feel like a fraud. I'm out there talking about oppression, how our power lies in not being silenced, and yet I'm too scared to tell some of my best friends who I really am. Because I don't want them to look at me differently." He grimaced at his words, and the urge to soothe him was almost overwhelming. "Which isn't even fair, because I know some of them want LGBTQ rights in Ethiopia as much as I do, but I'm still afraid. It's one thing to want something in theory, and quite another to have to confront it."

He took another sip of his water and looked toward the stage, where one of the women setting up was waving at him. After lifting his hand to her, he turned back to me. "For some of them I would no longer be Elias, their friend. I'd be the type of person they want to believe doesn't even exist in Ethiopia. There are people who think I'm the very symbol of the worst that colonialism did to our countries. They don't want to hear that we were always here." He looked weary, so different from the passionate, fiery man I'd grown accustomed to. "I shared those fears with Byron, and he used them as reasons to look down on me."

I had no idea why Elias was telling me all this, but I knew it couldn't be easy for him. I felt so fucking slighted for him. That asshole Byron had taken his secrets and used them to humiliate him. "I'm sorry you had to go through that, but I'm glad you didn't waste more of your time on someone who clearly didn't deserve you."

He dipped his head before he spoke. "Thank you. I felt so silly afterwards, like I should've known better. But I just wanted so much to have found someone that could *see* me."

I let out a long exhale, feeling his words in my bones. "I can relate to that on so many levels."

He raised his eyebrow at that and pushed his foot under the table so the tips of our shoes were pressed together. It was ridiculous and adorable how many ways he found to be close without really touching.

I felt like I had to share something with him too. I wanted him to know how much I valued his honesty. This night and the things we were saying to each other felt important, and I wanted to be as open with him as he'd been with me. "My ex broke up with me by letting me know he was going home to marry the girlfriend he'd been with the whole time we were together. I guess we both fell for people that didn't deserve us."

He seemed horrified on my behalf and tried to speak a couple of times, but in the end he just lifted his glass to clink it to my beer bottle. "To our battered hearts."

"To our stronger and *wiser* hearts," I replied.

As we smiled at each other, we heard the band getting ready to start playing. There was a DJ on stage mixing some music to get the crowd warmed up, and some of the musicians were fiddling with their instruments. After a moment, a second woman climbed on stage, and I decided she had to be the lead singer. She was wearing a bona fide rock star outfit, complete with brown leather pants, and with her makeup and hair, she could have stepped off the cover of *Rolling Stone*. When she grabbed the microphone, everyone in the room cheered.

I looked at Elias, impressed. "Wow, she's popular."

He shook his head in amusement. "You don't recognize her?"

I took a closer look as she scanned the crowd and waved back at some of the people in the audience. She spotted Elias and gave him a wink and smile. Then it finally dawned on me.

"Tsehay!"

She winked at me too, and I waved frantically as Elias blew her a kiss, which basically had me swooning.

I was so gone for him. It seemed that my stupid heart had learned nothing after Miguel, and decided it was a great idea to throw myself on the potential emotional landmine that was Elias. A man who was not only in the midst of making some major life decisions, but was also in the closet and on the rebound. *And* had been burned by a dude with a profile similar to mine.

Did any of this deter my thirst for him? Not even a little a bit.

Self-sabotage, thy name is Desta Joy.

I turned my attention to the band as the first notes of "Love Galore" by SZA sounded out through the space. I immediately stood up and pointed a finger at the stage while grinning at Elias, who had a matching expression on his face. "I have to be standing for this song. God, I love SZA."

He smiled and stood up too. Tsehay's voice was sultry and did the song justice. I looked around and noticed most of the people had started gathering around the stage, swaying to the music. Within a few seconds the entire place was singing along and belting out the chorus. It was one of those moments that can only happen when you are at a great gig, with everyone in tune to the music.

After SZA, they did a couple of Bob Marley and Amy Winehouse songs, and some Ethiopian pop music too. By the time the first set was done, I was only feet away from the stage, in a knot of people cheering and singing along with Tsehay and her band. Elias was standing right behind me, and it was the first time I truly noticed his height. He was taller than me, so the top of my head was right under his chin. I was consumed with the thought of how it would feel to lean into him. To feel the heat of this body against my back.

I wanted to touch him so badly that I kept coming up with excuses to rub up against him.

By the time the second set started, the place was packed, and pretty soon I did feel Elias's front pressed to my back. I looked up at him and he gave me a small smile as he ran a finger across my hip. Such a light touch, it could have been accidental. We were packed so close together. But with Elias against my back, a shiver ran down my spine at the contact. The impulse to turn around and push myself against him was so strong, I trembled.

When I looked up at his face, I could see my desire reflected there. As the band played and we moved to the music, we kept finding little ways to touch or brush against each other. Even a simple graze of his hand to my side felt erotic, and I was dizzy with wanting him.

After an hour of solid playing, the band was finally winding down and announced this would be their last song of the night. Elias bent down so he could whisper into my ear. "She always ends with the same song. That old Fugees cover of 'Killing Me Softly.'"

I grinned up at him as I heard the first notes. "I love that song."

As Tsehay sang the first verse, the entire place lost it. This song was an old favorite and so damn sexy, I *almost* turned around and wrapped my arms around Elias's neck. I was *feeling* him, this place, this music, this night with an intensity that had me on the verge of recklessness. Somewhere in the middle of the song we both turned to look at each other at the same time, and it was pretty obvious we had to get out of there, or commit a dangerous indiscretion. As the final notes of the song died out, Elias and I turned around in unison and headed for the entrance.

The ride in the elevator was pure torture.

We stood on opposite sides and stared intensely at the numbers indicating which floor we were on. I felt like my body was on fire for him. Elias didn't look like he was dealing any better; he kept pushing his fisted hands in his jacket, as if trying to keep himself from grabbing me.

Once outside, we power walked back to the car in silence. When we were finally inside, I turned to him and said in a breathless voice I barely recognized, "Would you come up to my place for a drink, or do you have to head home?"

He smiled at me and quickly ran his finger the side of my face. "Eshi, konjo, a drink sounds nice."

Never mind I had literally no liquids in my room other than water bottles, shampoo, and lube, but I nodded and pressed my face against the cool glass of the window as he pulled out on to the road. It was almost eleven and the streets were mostly empty except for the occasional person on the sidewalks, or a slumped figure wrapped in long white fabric, trying to keep warm.

Elias parked his car right outside the gate of the guesthouse. I used my keys to get us inside the compound, and soon we were climbing the stairs to my room. When I went to open the door, my hands were shaking. We'd both been quiet on the way over here, and now were about to do something that would change everything between us. I should've probably given that more thought.

I should've paused to consider my choices.

But as my trembling hands pushed open the door to my room, all I could think about was locking the door behind us so I could finally feel what I'd been dreaming about for weeks.

CHAPTER 11

As soon as we walked in, Elias turned to lock the door. We stood there for a few seconds, just looking at each other. It was like we were both trying to decide just how bad an idea this could potentially be.

In the end, I was the one who caved.

My heart was beating so fast, and I *was* scared, but not so scared to not get closer. I walked up to him, wrapped my arms around his neck, and kissed him. I felt the electricity of that kiss all the way to the tips of my toes. I sighed into his mouth while he grabbed my hips, crushing me against him. Not much had made sense in my life for so long, but this kiss, this man, I was certain of.

After a few short and fevered kisses, he lifted his hands, placing them on both sides of my face as he pried my lips open with his tongue. He licked in slowly, like he wanted to know me from the inside. I moaned and leaned in closer, bit his lip playfully, and got a surprised groan for my efforts. I felt the thrill of his tongue tangling with mine, our breaths mingling. Hot and hungry, and the sensation moved through me like wildfire.

He felt so good.

I couldn't get close enough, touch enough. Soon I had my hands down by his ass, squeezing hard, which got me a nip on the lip.

"You like that, konjo?" he breathed out, voice tight from lust.

I groaned as I tried to get closer. "I can't stop touching, and you smell so good. What is that?"

He made a husky sound, a mix between a laugh and a groan, and ran his lips down my neck while his hands wrecked my hair. I was so hard already, and when I grabbed his dick over his jeans, I felt it pulse in my hand.

"What did you say?" he asked between sucking on my Adam's apple and pinching my nipple through my shirt.

I moaned from the pulse of pleasure from his touch and struggled to recall what he was asking me about. "What? Uh, oh? Perfume." I sniffed him again and he laughed.

"Oh, it's Pasha—my sister got it for me. You like it?"

"Yes, and it was already impossible for me to focus whenever you were around, all hot and smelling good. Now that I know your kisses are fire and your tongue is fucking magic, I'm really concerned about my productivity."

He chuckled and made a grab for my cock, which was rock hard. "But I haven't shown you even a fraction of the things I can do with my mouth." He turned his head then and ran his tongue down the side of my neck, and I swear I blacked out for a second. "Or with my tongue."

"Oh god. You're going to kill me."

Another husky chuckle, and then his strong arms tightened around me. His eyes were like embers on my skin as he pressed a hand to the bulge in my jeans. "I want to taste you, Desta. I want to lick and suck you until you come in my mouth."

Holy shit.

I gurgled some kind of affirmative response as Elias took off his jacket before going down to his knees in front of me. In this light, his skin glowed. Bronzed with a bit of red on his cheeks from arousal, his lips bruised from my kisses. I wanted to eat him. I wanted to be the one on my knees for him.

I ran a finger over his eyebrows, which I still found distractingly perfect. "I could come from just looking at you like that."

"I promise this will be better." He grinned as he started undoing my fly. Once he had it open, he pulled the edge of my briefs aside so he could lick my balls, teasing me, flicking his tongue on the damp cotton covering my cock, but not taking it out yet.

"Baby," I whined. "Please. Take it out and suck me."

He made soothing sounds as he stroked my thighs, still not putting his mouth on me, and I was ready to beg. "Patience, konjo. Let me take my time. I've been dreaming about having you like this for weeks." He was breathless too, and that only made my own need that much stronger.

"You're not alone in that." I huffed as he pressed a thumb to my perineum. "I'm going to come," I said, feeling truly desperate.

He laughed, his eyes twinkling at how crazy he was making me, and slowly pulled my cock out. I was leaking and had made a huge wet spot on my underwear. He sucked on the head for a second, then pushed my briefs and pants down. He helped me out of my shoes next, and pretty soon I was half naked with my dick trying its best to get into Elias's mouth.

"You're so beautiful, Desta. I've imagined what you looked like. If your cock was going to be the same pretty pink as your lips. How it would feel to take you deep."

"Elias." I was begging and wasn't even sure for what.

He took me in hand and started flicking his tongue on the slit—light, fluttery touches that made every muscle in my body contract. It felt so good, and the way he kept squeezing my ass so his fingers brushed my hole was slowly driving me crazy. I wanted to just melt into the ground and plead for him to finish me off.

Then in one thrust he sucked me to the back of his throat. All I could do was pant and call his name while he teased my ass and swallowed around my dick. "I'm so close, you feel too fucking good."

He groaned and pulled off so he could lick my slit again, all while taking turns between teasing my hole and my balls. It was a full-on assault of my senses, and I knew I wouldn't be able to hold back very long.

I let out a long moan and grabbed his hair in warning. "I'm coming."

Instead of releasing me, he doubled down on my dick, and I felt his throat tighten on the head again as his finger pressed gently against my entrance. My whole body shook as an orgasm crashed over me. My breaths came out in pants as my groin and guts turned to liquid. "Baby, that feels so good. So good."

After a few seconds, I opened my eyes to see him staring up at me with a smug smile tugging at his lips. "I've been wanting to do that since we were on the road to Awassa. I had to stop myself from staring at your backside every time you jumped off the truck." He dabbed just a little bit of something from his lips and then popped the finger in his mouth, and my dick made a valiant attempt at reacting to the sight. "I knew you'd be delicious."

Fuck. He really was trying to kill me.

I touched his face and ran my thumb over his upper lip. "You have no idea how infatuated I've been since the moment I saw you."

He gave me that amused look I'd seen a few times whenever I paid him compliments. I tugged on his shoulder and he stood up. We were so close that I had to bend my head at an angle to look at him.

"I like your mouth," I said as I touched it. It was perfectly shaped, the skin just a bit darker than the rest of him. I parted his lips with my finger, and he bit me.

"Hey," I protested, using my other hand to tug on his thick curls. I could hold a fistful and not even get half of it. Everything about him was like that to me. Like there was so much of him I wanted to touch, to smell, and I'd never get to all of it. I felt greedy with Elias, wanted more of his time, more of his body. It was going to be a problem because I knew this couldn't last.

But I could compartmentalize like a champ. So I put all that drama aside and went down on my knees without a word. I found his eyes with mine, holding them as I moved down his body. Undid his jeans and nuzzled his cock through his boxers.

I licked him through his shorts and he hissed, a shiver coursing through him. I looked up and smiled. "What's that? Am I too much for you?"

He shook his head and grabbed my hair with one hand, his cock with the other. "I thought you wanted this," he said as he rubbed the tip of it against my lips. There was a bead of pre-come on it, and I stuck out my tongue again to lap it up.

He sucked his teeth as I went deeper. I loved how much he reacted to my touch; I wanted to make him crazy. Touch him until he lost control.

His shoes and jeans were off within seconds, and finally I had him naked, if only from the waist down. His cock was gorgeous. Uncut with a ruddy tip that was practically begging for my mouth. I ran my tongue from slit to base while Elias whispered encouragements. In one movement I took him as far down as I could. He made a choking sound and clenched his ass hard enough I could feel the muscles flexing where I was holding him.

"Oh, that's nice." He moaned as I did my best to take him all the way down to my throat. I looked up as I drew almost all the way out, leaving just the tip in my mouth.

In a breathless voice he said, "I'm not going to last. You're so good. Can you take me again? I want to see those red lips stretched as I fuck your mouth."

I gave a slight nod, took him all the way in, and hummed as I started sucking and jacking him in earnest. His thighs started to shake a bit, and soon his breath was coming fast. "I'm right *there*, konjo." Within seconds he was spilling down my throat as he panted my name. I swallowed everything he had and then brushed my lips against his thighs, resting my head against him. We stayed like that for a minute. Me kissing his stomach and thighs, him running his hands through my hair.

I stood and helped him out of his shirt without saying a word. He slipped mine over my head as I pulled him to my bed. I didn't ask him to stay the night, because I knew he couldn't. But I wanted to pretend, if only for a little while, that Elias and I could do this. That we could make love, then go to bed together. That he didn't have to go home and lie to his family about who he'd just been with.

I felt so far away from my life here. *I could pretend.*

In the place where I was supposed to be finding myself, I would lose myself in him.

* * *

THE SHEETS WERE cold when we got in the bed, and Elias pulled me against him so my back was flush with his chest. His skin was smooth and hot against mine, and his kisses on my shoulders made me shiver.

"I like how soft this is," he said running his hands through my chest hair. I didn't have a lot, but what I did have was mostly on my pecs. I had a stocky build, but Elias was still wider than me, and sitting like we were now, I felt enveloped by him. "I wondered how you would feel. You feel better than I imagined, and I had created very lofty expectations in my head."

I smiled, turning around so I could kiss him again. "I can't say this is unexpected on my part. I wanted to jump you from the moment I saw you."

He laughed and grazed his lips on the palm of my hand, which was such a ridiculously romantic thing to do. I would be hopelessly lost to this man in no time at all. "I was wondering if those looks you gave me in Awassa every time you had a couple of beers were just a coincidence. You would go like this." He did this squinty-eyed thing and said, "I was going to suggest you go to the eye doctor."

I balked and tugged on one of his curls. "Hey, watch it. That's my smolder."

He legit guffawed at that, "Like in the Disney movie?"

"Yes!" I wailed, which only sent him into another fit of laughter.

After he finally calmed down, he shook his head and looked at me like I was the cutest thing he'd ever seen. Then he grabbed the back of my head and kissed me until I was squirming against him. He pulled back, smiling. "You crazy farenji."

I backed away a bit, waved my hand between us and crowed, "Hey! It worked."

I always got fidgety when I felt I was under someone's scrutiny, like if they looked long enough they'd realize I was a fraud. That I didn't mean any of the things I was doing. But Elias looked at me like I was something worth understanding. As if he hadn't worked it all out yet, but what he could see, he liked a lot. I got closer and ran my hands over his chest, tucked my head right under his chin, and took a deep breath.

He sighed too and said, "I'm very glad to be with you here right now." Then he laughed in a way that wasn't exactly humorous. "It's also a little bit frightening. I've been thinking so much about Ari and Dante in the past few weeks."

I turned so I could look at his face. "I wondered what you thought about the book. You didn't say much when it ended."

He tightened his arms around me as he spoke. "Everything I felt after we finished it seemed too dangerous to say in the moment."

I nodded in understanding. "How does it feel now?"

He pulled me closer, and in a very serious voice said, "Too good to question."

I turned around to kiss him again, and lay there in his arms in silence. I mulled over everything that passed between us in the past few hours, how monumental it all felt. And there remained so much I needed to figure out.

I still had no idea what I would do about the job I was supposed to start once I got back to DC, or the acceptance in the NYU master of social work program. Worst of all, I didn't know how I'd tell my mother I didn't want to do this work. That I wouldn't follow in my dad's footsteps anymore. That I was selfish enough to break her heart.

CHAPTER 12

I woke up alone in the bed and heard movement around the room. When I turned a light on, I saw Elias sitting by the foot of the bed, putting on his shoes. My breath caught at the sight of his wide shoulders and back.

I walked on my knees to him and put my arms around his neck. "What time is it?"

He bent his head to kiss my hands, and that feeling like he could shake loose everything that felt constricting, spread through my chest again.

His voice cracked like thunder in my quiet room. "It's just before 4:00. I didn't want to wake you, but I need to get going. I take my mom to the market on Saturdays when I'm home."

I pulled back fast, worried I'd cause him to upset his mother. "Oh, okay. Don't want to get you in trouble with her."

He smiled at my reaction. "It's fine. I don't have a curfew. She just likes to get there early." He straightened from tying his shoes with a weary sigh. "I also wanted to slip out before the front desk staff gets in."

Right. Because it wasn't smart or safe to do this.

"Yeah," I said, not wanting to make things awkward.

He got up, pulling on his shirt as he walked to the door. I got out of bed and followed him, shivering in the chilly dawn. Before he opened it, he turned around and kissed me long and deep. "It's taking an enormous amount of self-control to leave this room when you're standing here completely naked."

I pushed up against him, not giving a fuck about looking needy, thirsty, or whatever, and bit his lip before I spoke. "Please tell me I get to do this again *soon.*"

He nodded sharply at that. "I'll be busy today. I have a few things to do with my family since I've been gone so long, but maybe tomorrow? I can take you up to Entoto Mountain—we can go for a hike and have lunch up there."

"That sounds good," I said, a bit disappointed that there was no mention of activities we could do in private, and then reminded myself he'd already take a huge risk by coming up here with me tonight.

I pulled on the lapel of his jacket and brought him down for one last kiss. "I have plans to see an old friend of my mom's today. She wants to go swimming at the Marquis. I've heard it's quite the place."

He nodded as he nuzzled my neck, making me want to jump him all over again. "It's very nice. The food is overpriced, but it's definitely a good place to spend the day relaxing." He turned to unlock the door. "Tomorrow then. I'll text you later to set a time."

I nodded and tried my best not to sound too whiny. "I'll see you then."

For a minute, we just stood there looking at each other. I wondered if, like me, he was feeling like we were about the burst the bubble. That once he left we'd be in the morning-after weirdness—the doubt, the secrecy, and the bullshit which would surely follow what we'd started tonight.

Neither of us said anything though, and I stood there shivering as he slipped out of the room and down the stairs, barely making a sound.

When I got back in bed, I wrapped myself in the sheets and pressed the pillow he'd been sleeping on to my face. The ache of not having him next to me felt too big, and I was too tired to think about how I'd complicated things for myself again.

* * *

I COULDN'T GO BACK to sleep after Elias left, and was wide awake at six a.m. Thinking that with the time difference it would only be after ten in the Ithaca, I decided to Skype my mom. I sent her a message on chat asking if she was up. She said yes right away and I instantly felt guilty, knowing she'd been waiting on me to call for weeks.

I opened the Skype app, and within a few seconds her face appeared on the screen. She seemed tired, but she had a big smile on her face. She'd gotten a pixie cut last year, which made her look sort of elfish, and despite everything, seeing her was comforting.

"Hey Mamí. ¿En qué estás?" I asked, trying to distract her from what I was sure were bleary eyes and sex hair.

She frowned and reached to touch the screen. "Hola, mijo, I was worried about you. Other than a few emails and that two-minute call when you got there, I hadn't heard from you. Are you in Addis?"

I'd emailed or texted her every other day since I'd gotten here, but my dad had died here on a job similar to the one I was doing. Granted, his death had nothing to do with the work or being in Ethiopia, but still I knew she would get anxious.

"Mamí, I've been in way more remote places than this, and you know Ethiopia is very safe. I emailed you the day before yesterday to tell you we were coming back to Addis and that I was fine."

She flipped her hand like an email every few days was not nearly enough. "I know, but the roads can be dangerous and they're so narrow. I worry!"

I shook my head and tried not to get on her case about her assuming nothing had changed in the more than two decades since she'd been here. "Mamí, that was like twenty years ago! The roads are fine. We got back without so much as a flat tire. The logistics coordinator for the project drove me, and he was a driver for the embassy for years. He's also the most responsible person on earth." My stomach lurched from the mere mention of Elias.

This seemed to appease my mother, though, and her face relaxed somewhat. "Oh good, I'm happy to hear you're with a good driver. Although I'm not surprised." She sighed wistfully and looked up like she was recalling a memory. "We had such good years there. Met so many wonderful people." After another sigh, she perked up. "Did you see Saba yet?"

I rolled my eyes at her question. "¡No, mujer, ya te dije! Like I mentioned in *my email*, I'll see her today. I wasn't sure how late we'd get back yesterday and didn't want to cancel on her."

"Okay, mijo," she said, smiling wide at the mention of her friend. Saba had been my mom's best friend when they lived here, and their friendship had not only survived, but thrived in the years since. Saba worked for the United Nations, and growing up I saw her almost every year when she'd go for meetings in New York City. She would always invite my mom and me to stay with her for the weekend, and we would take the bus from Ithaca to see her.

Those weekends with Saba were some of the best memories I had with my mom. Saba was a loyal friend to my family and, after my dad died, the only person other than my grandparents my mom and I could talk to who understood how hard it was for us without him.

Saba was a warrior, the kind of woman I sometimes wished my mom could be. So fierce, nothing brought her low. When Dennis, her husband, died a few years back, she'd told us not to come for the funeral, that she'd rather meet us in Germany. She said Dennis would've loved for her to take a holiday in his homeland with close friends and celebrate his life. So that's what we did. Saba did not let anything get the best of her.

I looked at my mom, who was still waiting for my answer, that fierce adoration which could be as comforting as it was stifling all over her face. I knew she'd done the best she could after my dad died, even though sometimes I wished so much of her happiness didn't depend on me.

"Mijo, where did you go?"

"Sorry, Ma," I said ruefully, as my mother's worried face stared at me from the screen. "I spaced out. Saba's coming to pick me up in a few hours and then we're going to a fancy hotel for the afternoon. After that I'm going to her house for dinner."

She gave me a thumbs-up like I was five. "Make sure you give her what I sent her. And don't forget your sunblock, papí. You're so light-skinned, just like your father. You burn in a minute." Hearing her, you wouldn't think I'd spent a good portion of the last year working in the Sudanese desert.

"Got the sunblock in my bag, Ma. They're right in there with my towel and floaties."

She hissed at my backtalk. "Fresco." She sounded amused, but I also didn't want to push it, so I shifted gears.

"How are things there, Mamí? Things okay with work? Jim?"

My mother had finally gone back on the dating scene two years ago. She'd been seeing a very boring and exceedingly nice man who worked some kind of finance job up at Cornell. Jim was from Connecticut, loved wine tasting and bird-watching, and seemed to be partial to cardigan and bowtie combos. But he doted on my mother, even though she took things at a snail's pace and agonized over any request he made to move their relationship forward.

She waved her hand, dismissing the poor guy. "He's good, and work is busy, lots of clients and training new staff same old, same old. That bitch Suzy is finally retiring, thank God. Mujer tan mala esa."

I cracked up at my mom's saltiness—she and her coworker Suzy had been nemeses for like, ten years, yet exchanged holiday cards religiously. My mother's explanation for this: "She's a bitch, but I still need to be polite."

I gave her a look and pushed her a little bit. "Madre. I'm glad Suzy won't be aggravating you for much longer, but tell me more about things with Jim." I pursed my lips at how flustered she looked. "What, are you getting shy in your old age?"

She balked at that and wagged her finger at me. "Mira, mucha-chito. Who're you calling old?" I chuckled, but she finally caved. "Ay, he's been saying he wants to get married, and I just don't know. It's too fast."

I sighed. "You're both sixty *and* you've been dating for almost two years. How long do you need?"

She tried to answer, but instead her chin quivered and her eyes watered, and my face felt hot with shame for pushing her. I rushed to reassure her, but she spoke before I could.

"I know I'm being silly, papí." She clicked her tongue. "Your dad's been gone for so long, but some days I wake up and I can still smell him." Her throat moved as she tried to choke down her tears, and I hated myself for starting this.

She wiped her eyes and slumped on the couch. "Jim's a good man and I know he won't wait forever, but I need more time."

I reached out my hand so I was touching the screen, and she stretched hers to touch the same spot. I closed my eyes, feeling the rapid heartbeat and breathlessness that happened whenever I saw my mother still in so much pain over losing my dad.

"Mamí, forget what I said. Take your time. I just want you to be happy."

She nodded and gave me a watery smile. "I know, papí, and I am. Now let's stop this sad talk. Go get ready to see Saba. Tell her I'll text her this week to set up a time to talk."

"Are you doing anything fun tomorrow? Are you and Jim hitting the winter market?"

She nodded and gave me that look of *I know what you're doing* whenever I tried to get her mind off of my dad.

"Yes, we're going shopping, and then we're getting together with his friends from the birding club." She rolled her eyes. "God help me." I cracked up at the look of horror on her face. But as much as she griped about Jim's hobby, the last few times I'd seen her, she'd woken me up before dawn to take me bird-watching with her. "At least it's at that new Caribbean restaurant that opened a few months ago. We need to go when you visit—the owner's Dominican." She delivered that news like the Obamas had just moved to her neighborhood. But she caught up to me soon enough. "Don't distract me, Desta. I was going to ask you something. Has that man called you? I talked to your Tía Lily and she said she saw the wedding announcement in one of the Santo Domingo papers. The nerve that little boy has after wasting your time for two damn years."

Oh man, if we went down this particular road, I'd be here until dinner. "No, I made it very clear to Miguel the last time we talked that I had nothing left to say to him." The finality in my voice was a new development I knew was at least partly related to a certain Ethiopian psychologist. "I doubt he's going to be calling me."

She looked primed to go on yet another rant about how Miguel was the embodiment of evil, and I was not in the mood. At least her earlier sadness was fully gone now and replaced by righteous fury. That'd definitely take her mind off my dad.

"I got to go, Mamí. I have to shower and get a little bit of work done before Saba comes to pick me up." I was probably going to take a nap, since I'd gotten very little sleep. Not that I regretted it in the slightest.

She nodded, but I could tell she was trying to get a read on my dismissal of Miguel, and we were *not* going there. "Okay, papí, bendición. Be careful. Love you."

My mother always told me to be careful, even when I was thousands of miles away and she literally had no control over what I did, but she had to get that in there.

"Bendición, Mamí, I love you too."

That blessing, or bendición, was also a must in every conversation with my mom. Despite the fact that neither of us had gone to a church for anything other than a funeral or a wedding ever since I could remember, I could not get off the phone without asking for a blessing. Who was granting said blessing was yet to be determined, but it had been our sign off my whole life.

This morning, with so much on my mind and knowing all the ways in which I was being reckless, her request to be careful felt like advice I should heed. Instead, I ignored all trepidation and checked my phone to see if Elias had sent a message.

When my stomach did a back flip from reading the message from Elias telling me he wished he could give me a good-morning kiss, I knew my common sense had no chance of winning this war with my dumbass heart.

CHAPTER 13

A few hours later I was standing outside of the guesthouse waiting for Saba. I smiled like a loon when I saw her drive into the compound. As soon as she stopped the car, I hurried up to the driver's side and opened the door to pull her into a hug.

She looked like royalty in a flowy emerald caftan and leather sandals, her braids in an intricate design, and her fingers and wrists full of silver jewelry. She was such a stunning woman. Whenever she visited us in New York, that first moment I spotted her in the crowd, I always paused to take her in. Even now in her sixties, she had the kind of elegance and poise that made people literally stop in their tracks.

I squeezed her tight, closing my eyes. "Saba, it's so damn good to see you."

She pulled back to give me the kind of thorough once-over only a tía could give. "Look at you. You're the perfect mix of your parents. So handsome. I'm so happy to have you here in your first home. Give me another hug, it's been too long." She brought me in for another squeeze. "Now that you're a grown-up and I can't lure you to New York City for weekend adventures, I never see you!"

I gave her a sheepish look, but didn't say anything about the possibility of me being in New York sooner than she thought.

She beamed at me again and started asking questions before I could get a word in. "Tell me about this new job. Fatima said you'll be running one of the units at the Aid USA headquarters. She's so proud of you. I'm proud of you too," she said, gently putting a hand on my face. "You've grown up so fine. Your dad would have been so pleased with what you've done."

There it was, the knife to the gut.

I smiled and nodded as I swallowed through the lump in my throat, as I always did whenever someone told me how I was carrying on my father's legacy. I let that weight sit right between my shoulder blades, looking for a way to give some kind enthusiastic answer.

But Saba was a wily woman.

After a moment, she gave me an assessing look, put her arm around my shoulder, and went right where I didn't want her to. "But what I should have asked was how *you* felt about it. Who cares about what two old women and the memory of a very-good-but-quite-dead man think? You're the one who has to live with it!"

Leave it Saba to lighten the mood with her dark-as-night humor.

I laughed and got in the car. "All right, old lady, buy me a beer at this fancy joint you're taking me to and I'll catch you up on my life."

She winked at me as she put the car in drive and headed out of the guesthouse. "I want all the gory details."

"Well, first there was the breakup with Miguel." I trailed off, knowing there would be a reaction.

Saba did not disappoint in her scorn for my ex. Her mouth twisted to the side at the mention of his name. "Fatima told me about that. He's the one who lost here. You don't need a man who can't see your worth."

I knew she meant it. Saba was not one to say things to be nice. If she said it, she believed it.

"Thanks." I realized after I'd said it that I didn't feel like talking about Miguel, so I veered elsewhere. "The job in DC is exciting, though," I said, forcing myself to sound enthusiastic. If I was an expert at anything, it was at telling my loved ones what they wanted to hear.

Saba looked at me like she suspected there was more there, but she didn't push.

We sat in silence, and after a few minutes, drove into what I assumed was the Hotel Marquis. I turned in my seat to get a good look at the majestic entrance of the hotel. "Wow. Someone did *way too much*," I said, awed by the enormous grounds and gorgeous gardens.

Saba chuckled as I took everything in. From the gate to the buildings, everything looked like something straight out of Vegas or Dubai. The entrance was a twenty-foot gilded metal gate, manually operated by white-gloved bellhops wearing red velvet jackets with gold embroidery. And that was only to get into the *parking lot.*

It only got swankier once we were inside. I stood in the lobby and turned around, gaping at all the marble and crystal. "Saba, this is *fancy.* Whatever happened to your rustic tastes?"

She smacked my shoulder as I turned in another circle. "Leave me alone, you brat. I'm old and like nice things now. Close your mouth and let's start walking to the pool so I can buy you a beer and something with no meat in it."

"Fine." I laughed and followed her through the patio leading to the pool. All the way down we saw breathtaking views of the mountains surrounding Addis. The place was gorgeous and so over-the-top. It was hard to reconcile with the fact we'd passed shanties only a few meters from the entrance. Expat life could give you whiplash sometimes. But I was not going to begrudge Saba for treating herself; she certainly deserved it.

When we got to the pool, we found two empty chaises and ordered some drinks and food. After a minute Saba turned to me and grabbed my hand, her face as serious as I'd ever seen it. "Desta dear, you know how much I love your father and your mother." She waved a dark brown hand in the air above her head. "Of all the people I've seen coming through my country to work, help, or whatever they tell themselves they do here, they're two of the precious few I not only liked, but respected."

Feeling unprepared for a big and heavy conversation, I tried a bit of teasing. "Did you bring me here to make me cry, Saba Aklilu?"

She gave me a rueful look, but carried on, unfazed. "Don't tease your Aunt Saba. I'm serious. Fatima is still one of the few people I trust with my deepest and darkest secrets, *but* she never did know how to manage projecting her grief onto you." She pursed her lips, a sad but fond smile on her face as she talked about my mother. "Your father was a man who believed in following his dreams. He did what he wanted, and what he felt had value, but mostly he did what *made him happy*. You've got to be happy, konjo."

And now I was blushing because that word would now forever be connected to Elias and the incredibly hot things he could do with his mouth.

Saba was on a roll, though, and before I could interject, she said the words I hadn't realized I desperately needed to hear. "If that job isn't what you want, don't take it because you think it's what would make your mom happy."

I tried to look away, but she pulled my face back gently. "And really, as far as that young man who left you—even though it's hard to see now, he did you a favor. You didn't want to invest more time in someone who was so careless with your heart."

I sighed, thinking the job was a lot harder to grapple with right now than Miguel. Granted, it was probably because I'd already gotten myself involved with someone even more likely to fuck me up, but I didn't need to go down that sinkhole right now.

Instead, I tried to focus on this moment with Saba. "With Miguel, it's like I was telling Elias." I waved a hand as I explained. "He's the logistics coordinator for the project I'm working on." She gave me a weird look, since I'd just implied I was talking about my boyfriend troubles with a colleague, but I kept going. "At this point it's more humiliating than anything else. Like I can't trust myself to know who really cares for me and who just wants to play me."

I sat up and looked at the pool while I spoke. I didn't know how to say the next part. "And about the job, I don't know, Saba. Mamí would be so hurt. You know that."

"She may be hurt, but I also know that life goes by in a blur. If you know this work doesn't fulfill you, find what does and go after it."

I was grateful for Saba's encouragement, but I was just not there yet. I grabbed my cold bottle of beer from the little table between us and took a long sip. "Thanks for saying all that, really. For now, I'm happy to be here hanging out with my second favorite old lady."

She balked and I cracked up. "Naughty boy! I'm going to make you pay for your own beer if you keep calling me old!"

Saba let things go after saying her piece and started telling me a funny story about a coworker. By the time the server came with our food, I was wiping the tears from my eyes. We grabbed our sandwiches and chewed in silence for a few minutes, enjoying the perfect weather and delicious food. I was picking at the fries on my plate when Saba looked over at me. "So, what's the plan for the next few weeks?"

"Work," I said, trying hard not to sound too excited about the prospect of a few more weeks with Elias. "We have to run another survey. I think we'll be out there for another three weeks. I have about ten days on the back end to do some travelling once we're done. I was hoping to go to the Simien Mountains and Gondar. Elias said he knows of a few good places that plan tours for people travelling alone."

She nodded, then gave me a look that made me nervous. "Tell me about this Elias. It's the second time I've heard about him in twenty minutes."

I knew I was blushing again, but the image of Elias on his knees with my cock stretching out his lips was going to have that effect on me for a while.

I cleared my throat and looked at the deep end of the pool, which had suddenly become extremely fascinating. "Umm, he's part of the team. For this project. In the field. I mean—he's with Aid."

"Uh-huh." Saba was not buying it. "And you're on very friendly terms, I see."

I could go with that. We *were* on friendly terms.

"Yeah, he's great." I grinned because I couldn't help it. "He's a psychologist. Actually, he's considering going to New York for a PhD at Columbia. I mean, he got in, but he deferred and is deciding whether to go or not." And that was not making me fret, and I was not wondering what it would be like for Elias to be at Columbia while I went to NYU.

I would never do that because I wasn't delusional.

Saba dipped her head approvingly. "Ambitious, but not too proud to do a less fancy job while he gets himself through school. I like him already."

As Saba said that, I thought of how meticulous Elias was about getting the supplies ready for us while we were in the field. The careful way in which he approached everything. And before I knew it I was gushing about him to Saba.

"He's great at his job too. There was not a single supply or emergency he wasn't prepared for in the field. Even when Sam, one of the expats, majorly fucked up and we had to scramble to go out on the field without him." I narrowed my eyes, thinking about what an asshole Sam was that day. "Elias just took over one of the teams without missing a beat."

Saba was looking at me with a smirk on her face. Knowing her, she was probably plotting some kind of romance, despite the many issues that could bring me in Ethiopia.

I rolled my eyes at her. "Saba, stop scheming."

She scrunched her eyebrows and tried for an innocent expression.

I wasn't buying it. "I'm not even sure what's going on with your eyebrows and eyes right now, but if it's some corny idea about me and Elias, stop it. It's not happening." I actually clapped my two hands together, because yeah, we needed to shut all this shit down.

She just laughed at my protests. "I'm not doing anything with my eyebrows. He just sounds like a nice man." She snapped her fingers then, and the wide smile that followed set my alarms off. She was up to something. "Actually, he sounds like a great fit for a program I'm hiring for at the moment."

As soon as she mentioned a job, I got fidgety. Elias was supposed to come to the States for a PhD, where I could get to know him better.

Riiiight, all under control here.

I tipped my head to the side and tried not to glare at her. "Well, he's thinking about school in the States. I'm not sure if he's the right guy for that."

Oh man that was the face of someone who had my number.

"Uh-huh. You forget I've known you your whole life, Desta Joy. Don't think you can fool me." She waved a finger in my direction. "You like that man."

I threw my hands up in exasperation and laughed. "What's not to like? He's hot as hell. I mean, God, Saba, he's so fucking beautiful. His eyes, and that mouth." I sighed. "His hair is on the long side." I shook my head while she grinned at me. "Just curls everywhere, which for some reason I find intoxicating. Everything about him is so damn sexy."

I slouched against the chaise, closing my eyes. "It's a problem, to be honest."

Saba's voice was pure mischief. "You took that man to bed already, and you'll do it again."

I snapped my eyes open at that and had to chuckle at the glee in her voice. "*Saba!* Oh my God. Why are you so shady? Seriously, you're like a second mom. I can't talk about this stuff with you."

She laughed at me again. "It's true, and you know it."

I put my hands over my face, muffling my words as I spoke. "Can we stop talking about Elias, please?"

I looked at her through my fingers, and she finally took pity on me. "Fine. Tell me about your plans for your days off. I can recommend some new places."

I slumped on my chaise dramatically and raised my hands in supplication. "Thank God."

Saba shook her head and looked at me like I was an adorable mess. After that, the afternoon passed without any more intense conversations.

By the time we were drying off and heading to the dressing rooms, the sun was setting. As we walked to the showers, Saba looked at me, her face serious. "Desta, why don't you invite Elias over to the house for dinner? It'll just be you and me."

I stopped in my tracks and stared at her, freaking out a little. "Oh

111

no. I'm not going to be Mr. Needy and invite him over less than twenty-four hours after I had him—"

I quickly covered my mouth before I said something that would be cause for mortification until the end of my days.

Saba clucked, a hand on her hip. "I already told you I knew you'd taken him to bed. What's the harm in inviting him to the house? It's just dinner. Besides, you're both adults, and my dear, we *are* still in Ethiopia. You won't have many chances to spend time with him in a place where you can flirt to your heart's content."

"Saba." My fake whining was next-level. "You don't even know if he's gay! *I* never said he was, and besides, there's *nothing* going on."

She looked at me like I was the most pitiful thing on earth. "Invite him anyway. Like I said, he sounds like a good fit for this new program I'm hiring for. This could be a good opportunity for him."

"You're shameless. Fine, I'll text him even though he said he'd be busy today."

She gave me a thumbs-up, already walking off. "Great. See you in the lobby, dear." She headed into the ladies' dressing room as I took my phone out of my pocket, trying to ignore the butterflies in my stomach as I typed a message.

Desta: Hey, what are you up to? Still busy with your mom?

Elias: Hey *smiley face emoji* No, we got back some time ago, just watching TV with my niece. Did you have a nice afternoon?

For some reason, the image of him watching a cartoon movie or something else equally adorable with his niece made me feel all mushy. For all I knew, she was twenty-five years old.

Desta: What are you watching?

I was text flirting now.

Elias: Tangled! LOL After last night I wanted to see it. She's six, so it did not take a lot of convincing to get her to watch with me.

I was officially obsessed.

Desta: Are you trying to copy my smolder? Because I can tell you right now, it won't work.

Elias: *wink emoji* I don't need the smolder to get what I want.

Aaaand I now had an erection... Deep breaths.

Desta: Wow. Someone's a little too sure of himself.

His response? The kiss emoji.

Desta: So, actually, I was wondering if you were up for coming to dinner with me and my friend.

Elias: Oh? Someone from Aid?

Desta: No, it's my mom's friend. It'll be at her house, but I was telling her about you and she said I should invite you over. She's making me a full Habesha feast, not sure if you're up for it??

Elias: Unlike you, I can ALWAYS eat injera. *smiley face emoji* That sounds nice actually, my mom is going to my aunt's with my sister and I was hoping to get out of having to go too.

My insides flipped over in excitement, which *should* have concerned me.

Desta: Excellent. We're at the Marquis now but should be heading to her house soon. She lives in Jacros. I can give you more details once I get them from her.

Elias: I know Jacros, I am not too far actually. Just by Meganagna.

No clue where that was, but great.

Desta: I'll text you specific directions soon. Does 7:30 work?

Elias: Eshi Desta. See you then. *smiley face*

Oh man, I was nauseous with excitement from a smiley face emoji. It was like I had lost all ability to control my fool head.

CHAPTER 14

By the time we got to Saba's, I was questioning every decision of the last twenty-four hours. Right at the top of the list was packing holey jeans and a ten-year-old Cornell sweatshirt for my change of clothes. I looked like the token Latino frat bro at a kegger.

I tugged at the hem of my sweatshirt, utterly disgusted. "Why did I not bring something decent to wear?"

Saba looked up at me while opening a bottle of wine and smiled. "What are you so worried about? I thought you weren't interested in this man."

"Obviously I was lying, Saba!" I moaned, and flung myself on her couch. "You *know* I like him! Ugh, now you made me say it!"

She cackled and passed me a glass, patting me on the shoulder. I sipped morosely as I looked at the clock on the wall. Elias would be here any minute. I'd texted him instructions about thirty minutes ago, which was how long he said it would take him to drive over.

I heard a car pulling up to the gate of the house and saw Saba's guard come out to open it. I quickly got up to look and saw Elias's Corolla pull into the big gravel driveway. I went out to meet him while Saba sat on her couch, looking amused.

"Looks like your guest's here." She was having a little too much fun with this, but I didn't have the bandwidth to come up with a snappy comeback. So I left my wine on her coffee table and went out to meet Elias.

He got out of the car with a bottle of wine in his hand, and once again took my breath away. This time he was wearing dark gray chinos and a bright red sweater, with a gray linen scarf around this neck. He looked like some sort of bohemian poet, and I wanted to kiss him so badly.

He walked up to the porch where I stood waiting for him, and we pressed our shoulders together in greeting. He pulled back and peered inside, but his expression changed to one of surprise when he saw Saba through the window. After a second, he shook himself and passed me the wine, eyes almost bulging out of his head. "You didn't say your friend was Saba Aklilu!"

I looked over my shoulder, confused by how freaked out he sounded, but found Saba placidly sipping wine and doing something on her phone. "Oh, I guess I didn't, but yes, that's her. Do you know her?"

He looked at me as if I was out of my mind. "No, but I know *of* her! She's a very well-known person in Ethiopia. She's sort of one of my heroes, actually." Well, that was interesting. "She's been a fierce advocate for women's and children's rights for decades, and lately she's been talking about LGBTQ rights too." He had a look of complete awe on his face when he said that. "She's fearless. I go to see her speak whenever she comes to the university."

It didn't occur to me Elias might have known Saba. I knew she was a well-respected figure here, but for me she was like an aunt. It was wild that he was this starstruck by her.

"Just say hello," I told him with an encouraging smile, completely charmed by his shyness and excitement. "She's looking forward to meeting you. I told her about your research."

He gave me a panicked expression. "You did?"

I rolled my eyes because he was too freaking cute. "Yes, she thought it was really interesting." I grabbed his hand and tried to pull him toward the door. "Come on, let's go in."

He didn't move, and when I looked back he was giving me that intense look he did sometimes, his lips slightly turned up on the corners. My heart raced and I resisted moving closer while we were still outside. It was hard, though.

"Why are you looking at me like that?"

"How else could I look at you, konjo?" His tone was completely matter of fact.

He was going to kill me.

My thoughts must have shown on my face because he winked at me and tugged on my hand. "Let's go inside."

* * *

SABA AND ELIAS got on like a house on fire, and within minutes they were in an intense conversation about the history of the fight for women's rights in Ethiopia that lasted all through dinner.

While we all took bites from the amazing spread of food on the table, Saba paused to look at me, then turned to ask Elias a question. "So, Elias, what do you think is the role of men in the fight to end misogyny in our country?"

He took the bite of food he'd had in his hand and sat back, chewing and thinking.

"I want to challenge Ethiopian men to be a part of our liberation from all the harmful constructs oppressing women in this country. It isn't right and it isn't fair to expect them to once again carry the burden of fixing what they didn't break."

Saba beamed at me, then pointed at him. "Good answer."

I smiled at her approval and sat there quietly, thinking about the certainty in Elias's answer. I'd never felt so passionate about anything. Elias spoke with such fire, like he believed every word he said. He was certain he could make a difference. I couldn't even tell my mom I didn't want to take a job I knew I'd hate, and had no clue if my other plan was any better.

It was a privilege to do the work I did, yet I had never felt the passion with which Elias spoke. Never felt like I was an important part of it.

I noticed a pause in the conversation and Saba's voice wrenched me out of my thoughts. "Desta, where did you go? I asked you a question."

"Oh, I'm sorry, what did you say?" I sounded more than a little distracted.

She gave me a worried look. Elias did too. "Elias said you're planning to hike up to Entoto tomorrow. That sounds like fun."

That perked me up because another day with Elias sounded like everything I needed right now. "Yes, I'm looking forward to it."

Elias squeezed my thigh under the table and turned to Saba, one of those perfect eyebrows raised. "So how was Desta as a kid? Was he always so excitable?"

I protested, trying to look put out. "Excitable? What am I, a puppy?"

He was having too much fucking fun torturing me. "No, no. It's just you seem to get so happy about new things. It's very cute." He made the word *cute* longer than it needed to be and gave me a mischievous look.

Saba looked between us, her face in an expression which had me bracing to be utterly embarrassed. "He was always such an emotionally open child. Even as a teen when most kids are so prickly. I'd go to New York for a visit, and after a whole year, I'd be unsure if he'd be interested in this old friend of his mom. But the minute he saw me, he'd run right into my arms and tell me how much he missed me, and how beautiful I looked."

Her eyes were so soft I actually felt a lump in my throat. "Desta always could share what he was feeling without shame. That is one of the many things that make him such a special man."

I rolled my eyes at her, knowing she'd get a kick out of it, and she laughed, pointing at me. "See what I mean!"

Elias beamed at her and looked primed to ask more questions, but before he could, I put my hands up, desperately needing out of this conversation. "Time out. Please, let's finish eating." I waved my hand over the table. "We can't waste all this delicious food."

Elias leaned closer and ran his hand over my leg again, making my entire body heat up. "Eshi, I'll stop asking questions."

I sighed, working to keep my feelings under control. "Okay."

Saba shook her head in amusement and went back to eating while I asked Elias about the hike to Entoto.

We finished dinner and went back to the living room to relax. While Elias and Saba talked Ethiopian politics some more, I got up to get a glass of water in the kitchen. I looked over my shoulder as I walked away, wanting to catch a glimpse of him as he talked. He took such care with what he said, and when he heard something particularly interesting, he would lean in and give his complete attention. Every once in a while, he'd grab the ends of his curls and squeeze like he was wringing out the emotion the words raised in him.

When I came back to the living room, Saba and Elias suddenly stopped talking. I tried to make a joke out of it as I sat down next to Elias. "Oh, don't worry, keep going. I don't mind people saying how handsome I am in front of me."

To my surprise Elias put his arm around me, pulled me close, and kissed the tip of my nose, because obliterating me seemed to be his goal for the night. "You know you are, konjo."

I blushed again and looked from him to Saba—who seemed completely unfazed by the display of affection—before opening my mouth. After a moment I asked, "What *were* you two talking about?"

Saba laughed and said, "We were just saying that it's getting late and you two have a long day tomorrow."

"Riiiight, and that's all you said."

Elias laughed and got up, pulling me with him. "I should get going, but I can drive you home."

I nodded and moved to grab my bag from where I'd put it by the door. Saba got up to see us off. "Stay safe out there, my dear."

Then she turned to Elias, squeezing his shoulder. "Take good care of him for me."

He dipped his head, a serious look on his face. "Eshi."

She gave him a kiss on each cheek and a *really* tight hug.

As Elias went to get the car started, I said goodbye to Saba. She held my face and said, "I like him for you. He's a brave man. Honest."

"Saba! I'm not here trying to find a boyfriend. Also he's super in the closet to his family and wants to be here, in Ethiopia, a place I love so far but won't be living in. And why I am even thinking of living places? Ugh, okay, I'm going."

She shook her head like I was talking nonsense, and I moved in for a last hug before heading out. I got to the car to find Elias beaming at me, and immediately everything felt okay again.

"Get in, konjo, so we can get you home. I still need my goodnight kiss."

CHAPTER 15

Elias parked outside and walked into the guesthouse with me. We hadn't talked about him coming up, but I didn't make a thing out of it and led the way to my room. We both hesitated in the doorway, and after a second I felt bold and pulled him in by the hem of his shirt. Once inside with the door locked, I pressed against him and stuck my nose in the crook of his neck. He always smelled so fucking good.

He immediately slid both his hands inside my briefs, one kneading my ass hard, the other looking for my hole. I moaned as he ran his thumb over it, just a touch, then pushed in. "I haven't stopped thinking about this."

I gasped, biting his neck. "I want more."

He growled, turning his head to get at my mouth. I let out a tortured groan as he sucked on my tongue hard and kept grazing the tips of his fingers over my hole. I was so turned on, and there was no way I could stop until I came. Until we both did.

Elias pulled back and his face was flushed. "Take your jeans off and put your hands against the wall. I want you to jerk off while I play with your ass."

Holy shit I did not see this toppy Elias coming at all, but I was here for it. "You have the best ideas," I said breathlessly.

"I'm waiting." He said with a stern note to his voice that made my dick impossibly harder. Elias was always so serious and proper, but this demanding side of him was hot as fuck. I did what he said, and in two seconds flat I had my hands up against the wall, legs spread, ass pushing out, having a hard time not humping the air.

Elias came up behind me without saying a word, and I could feel his cock through his trousers as he thrust hard against my ass. It took all I had not to beg him to fuck me. I was burning up for him—his breath on my neck, the possessive way he ran his hands over me, like he couldn't get close enough.

Suddenly I felt his hand come up my chest, and I legit panted. "I want to hear you scream for me, Desta. Tell me how much you like it when I touch you." He pinched my nipple hard and then rubbed it with his thumb. At this point words were getting hard to process, but what he was doing to me had me begging for more.

"I love how you touch me. I want your fingers in me."

With his other hand he pulled down my briefs, then pried open my cheeks. The feeling of being exposed like that combined with the cold air in the room hit me like a bolt of electricity. His touch consumed me, took over every one of my senses.

"You like this?" His voice was pure sex.

"Oh God." I started pushing my ass back on his hand, wanting, *needing* to feel more.

Elias lifted one hand to my mouth, hissing in my ear when I tongued his fingers. "Get them wet. Show me how you're going to suck my dick when I give it to you."

It was so dirty and I was so fucking into it.

He came closer to me, his mouth pressed to my ear. "You're making me want to give you my cock right now, you're sucking on those fingers so good." My ass clenched at the thought, but he shook his head, adding a third finger, which I took greedily. "No, I'm going to fuck you with these first. Make you come, then use your come to jerk off."

"Ungh, I may blow from just you talking."

His laugh was sinful, like he knew I had no idea what I was in for. "I want to see my come all over your ass, Desta."

I shuddered out a breath and sucked hard on his thumb. After a moment, he stepped back, and with one hand he spread my ass again and pushed his thumb in just a little bit. I was so close to coming that I was sure if he touched my cock I'd explode.

"Do you have lubricant?" he asked, his voice tight as he ran the pad of his finger over my rim. "I can't wait to see my fingers moving in and out of you."

My knees buckled, because between his hands on me, in me, and the things he was saying, I was having a hard time staying upright. I shook my head, trying to remember what he'd asked.

Lube. Right.

I was so desperate I'd probably be fine with him fingering me dry, but I nodded, pointing at my bedside table. "It's in the drawer."

I'd bought the lube on a whim as I prepared for my trip, but being around Elias had me jerking off on a daily basis, so I was grateful I'd gone for the full-size bottle.

He hurried to the bed and was back within seconds. I turned my head to see him coating two fingers with the silky gel, and my ass clenched again, needing them inside me already.

"I've been wanting to touch you like this since I saw you in those little shorts you run in." He massaged my rim as he whispered filthy things in my ear, making every nerve ending light up.

"That feels so good, baby. Give me more, please, I'm so close."

He slid in the first finger, pushing in gently until he found my spot. I practically wept from the sensation as he grabbed my cock and started stroking me just like I needed it.

"More of what, konjo?" he teased.

I shook my head and pushed hard against the two fingers he was now using to drive me fucking crazy. He took that as a cue and started working my dick in earnest.

I could feel the orgasm building fast. When he lightly brushed his fingernail against my slit on the upstroke, my legs buckled, pleasure flooding me. I felt the tightness starting between my ass and my groin when I was about to come.

The orgasm slammed into me so hard I couldn't make words. Elias stroked me through it, holding me up. When I was completely wrung out, he ran his thumb over my sensitive cock one last time and pulled his fingers out of my ass. Before he was fully out, he ran the pads of his fingers over my hole as he bit and sucked on my shoulder.

I was so over-sensitized, tremors were running up and down my body, and I knew the only reason I was still upright was because he had me. Elias kept kissing and tasting as he rubbed the head of his cock against my ass.

"I love your ass, Desta," he practically growled into my ear. "I want to see my come all over it."

I was totally blissed out from my orgasm, but his voice against my ears and his cock painting my ass with his pre-come had me so worked up, I was practically vibrating.

"Do it, baby." I pushed back and heard the slap of his hand as he worked himself. After a moment his breath became shakier and he let out a long moan as wetness splashed all over my back and ass.

Elias slumped on me and mumbled something in Amharic while he nipped and licked my neck and shoulders again. I could feel his hands sliding over my back. I turned to look at him, and his face was pure mischief. "I will lick the come off you next time."

"You're really fucking dirty." I couldn't help the admiration in my voice. The man's mouth was filthy, and I was truly obsessed.

He kept his eyes on my back, that wicked smile still on his lips. "You bring it out in me, konjo. Come, let's move to the bed."

He dragged us both over, and as I got under the covers he took his pants and shoes off, before getting in with me. We lay there for a few minutes, tangled in each other, my head against Elias's chest. Being with him was so intense, every moment magnified. Maybe it was this place—Ethiopia and its magic. Or maybe it was me once again moving too fast. Still, I couldn't deny the way he made me feel. Like everything made sense in his arms.

After a few minutes, I dislodged myself from him and sat up. "I need to get cleaned up. I feel like we're going to get stuck together."

He chuckled and pulled me down for another kiss before letting out a long sigh. "I should probably head out soon, too."

Right, because he was taking a risk even coming up to my room with me, let alone trying to sneak out at all hours of the night.

I didn't say anything and went to the bathroom for a washcloth. After a few minutes, I came out with a damp towel for him. As soon as I saw his face, I knew something bad had happened. The smile on his lips from just a few minutes ago was gone, his brow knitted with worry at whatever he was seeing on his phone. "What's wrong?"

He looked over like he was surprised to see me there, as if in the time I'd been in the bathroom, he'd forgotten where he was. He was busy tugging on his pants and looking at his phone, which was on the bed lighting up with notifications. "My father's in the hospital. I had my phone turned off, so I didn't see the messages until now."

I opened my mouth, but nothing came out. I felt like shit for keeping him away from his family, and terrified for him. Instantly I had worst-case scenarios flooding my head—of his dad being dead, of him not getting there in time. I was trying hard to breathe and not having much luck when I felt firm hands tighten around my arms.

"Desta."

I turned my face up to him and saw him looking down at me with worry. I had to get it together. His dad was sick and I didn't need to make it about me. I tried to shake off my own baggage about my dad and focused on him.

"I'm sorry. Of course you should go." I tried to sound normal. But I heard the tremor in my voice.

I distracted myself by putting on some clothes as he finished getting dressed. My mind was racing, thinking of all the ways him being here was a problem. The thought of Elias not being there for his dad because he'd been here with me sucked the air out of my lungs. I took a deep breath, and then another, trying to ground myself. And when I finally spoke, I sounded marginally less freaked out. "Was your family able to get to the hospital since you have the car?"

"My mom and my sister's husband have cars." His voice was calm and steady, and he'd clearly noticed I was having some kind of a meltdown.

"Oh, right." Now I felt like an idiot. I looked up at him and realized he wasn't making a move to leave. He closed his eyes standing by the door, as if he were preparing himself for whatever he'd face when he left my room.

He exhaled loudly as he buried his face in my hair, and I tightened my arms around him. If he needed someone to lean on for a moment before going to deal with a family crisis, I could fucking get my shit together and at least give him that.

After a minute, Elias spoke. "My mom and sister are with him. The hospital is close to here, and there's not much traffic at this time. I'll get there in a few minutes."

"Okay. Take the time you need," I said, lifting my watch to read the time. I realized it was later than I thought.

"Besides, being here with you helps."

I tried to smile at him, but I was still having a hard time calming down. My heart was beating out of my chest, and I was convinced Elias would not get to his father in time. But he'd told me it was fine, and I needed to respect that. "Do you know what's wrong?"

He tried to smile, but couldn't manage it. "My father's ill a lot. He has some heart problems, but he also suffers from—"

He shook his head like he was trying to figure out what to say, but in the end he just turned his face so his mouth brushed my neck, and we stayed like that for a few seconds. Soon he was moving again. He sighed heavily as he unlocked the door, and I could feel the apprehension coming off him in waves.

Once we were out by his car, without thinking I made a move to touch his hand. He flinched. Then I remembered where we were. This wasn't my room, or even Saba's house—we were out on the street. Anyone could walk by and see us.

"Sorry."

Elias nodded and smiled, but it didn't reach his eyes. "It's all right, konjo."

A feeling of dread settled in my stomach like something important had changed in the last few minutes, and we wouldn't get back the ease we'd had with each other only a half hour ago.

Hearing him use the endearment did something for my nerves, but I was still feeling out of sorts. "I hope your dad is okay."

"Me too."

I saw him drive off, then walked into the guesthouse, worried for Elias and his family. I also had the feeling that the bubble we'd been in, where we pretended Elias and I could be lovers, had just burst.

CHAPTER 16

After stopping myself from trying to text Elias for the third time in the hour after he'd left, I decided I desperately needed a talking-to. I had to check in with Lucía, because if anyone could get me off the bullshit I was on right now, it was her. I opened the Skype app on my laptop, hoping she was around.

DestaJoyWalker: Code Red. CODE.RED.

Lucía.Woods: WTF? Please tell me you're not skyping me after engaging in poor sexual choices.

DestaJoyWalker: OF COURSE I AM!!!!!!

Lucía.Woods: DON'T YELL AT ME!

DestaJoyWalker: I'm calling you!

I clicked on the video call icon, and within seconds she came on the screen.

She looked at my obvious case of "I just got railed" hair and shook her head. "Wow, you really went to town on that dick, huh? Dude was pulling hard on that cowlick of yours." Her mouth was twitching from trying not to laugh.

"Hey!" I said, while trying to pat down the spikes of hair that were standing up every which way. "First of all, I didn't give him a blowjob. Second, my cowlick has been a lot tamer since high school."

She cackled, and I could tell it hadn't escaped her that I failed to deny my sex hair.

"It's not that bad! You're such a jerk," I said with a laugh.

That just made her bust up even harder. "Oh my God, you're such a mess. Cute, but a mess. Okay seriously, though, what were you up to? I've got time. Moe's down at the studio space doing their thing."

I smiled at that. Luce's partner was an incredibly talented sculptor and would go work on their stuff every weekend. "Oh, I can't wait to see what they're working on."

She nodded, an adoring look all over her face. She only got that when Moe came up.

Luce had always been a wild woman. She fucked whoever she wanted and never took anyone she was with too seriously. She just played. But as soon as she met Moe, she knew. When she first told me about them, she sounded so certain about what she felt. I couldn't help thinking that I felt that same certainty about Elias, even if it was fucking self-destructive and idiotic.

"So what's this SOS about?" Now that I had all her attention on me, for the first time in our friendship, I paused. I didn't want to share too much. The moments I'd had with Elias already felt precious, like they'd shatter if I didn't handle them with care.

I realized I'd been quiet for a while, and when I glanced at the monitor I saw Luce staring at me with a funny look. "Babe, you look pretty serious right now."

I covered my face with my hands and groaned. "I could fall in love with this guy, Luce."

At this point she would usually make a joke about how my need to be "involved" was pathological. She didn't this time, though. She looked at me carefully and asked, "Who is it?"

"It's Elias, the logistics coordinator for the project I told you about when we talked after I got here." I sighed. "He's amazing. I want him so much, and not just because he's gorgeous and turns me inside out just from saying my name. He's so noble and passionate about everything."

"Okay, hon." She put her hands up, and I could tell she was trying hard not to lecture me. "I don't want to sound like I don't take your feelings seriously, but you do this. You meet a guy, decide you want him and you make it your mission to have him fall for you. Sounds like Elias is a great guy, so be careful with your heart *and* his, all right? You're only there for a few more weeks, and when you get like this, hell-bent on getting that connection…you make *promises.*"

I looked at her, feeling something heavy in my chest. It hurt to hear her say it. But she was right. I always did this, went in too fast and too hard. Convinced myself it was what I needed, and ended up either disappointed or heartbroken. But that didn't mean I didn't know what I was feeling right now. That I couldn't recognize that the things I felt for Elias were totally different than anything else I had before.

"Luce, I think this time it's different," I said, smiling helplessly when I thought of how good things felt with Elias. "I can just *be* with him. It feels so good and safe. I don't feel the need to be two steps ahead, dictating where we go next. I'm just happy to be there. He's so fucking brave too. Tonight we were at Saba's and he just grabbed my head and kissed me. Right in front of her." It was crazy to think that only happened a couple of hours ago.

"I know it doesn't seem like much, but doing that here openly is a risky thing, and he did it for me." I felt so fucking stupid and desperate, grasping at straws to make her understand that this was the real deal. "God, it sounds so corny when I say it, but it felt so good for someone to want me like that. So much he was willing to take chances. No one has ever done that for me."

Lucía was so clearly worried for me that I wanted to hide. "It's not stupid, Des. It's great," she said firmly. Her expression changed and she waved her hand in the direction of her laptop. "Forget all the shit I said. Enjoy him. Enjoy the trip. You *deserve* it. What I want is for you to be happy. Full stop. You do what you need to do, no matter what. I'm here always. You know that."

"Thank you." That was it. No more lecturing, no judgment. She let me know how she felt, but in the end she was happy to see me happy.

After that our conversation veered to my plans for the next weeks and my talk with my mother. I went to sleep feeling anxious about Elias and his family, but also determined to enjoy the time I had with him before we were both inevitably forced to focus on our obligations.

* * *

HE WASN'T COMING.

I woke up to a text from Elias saying he wouldn't be able to take me to Entoto. My stomach clenched as I read the message. I agonized, wondering if his dad had been having a heart attack while he was messing around with me.

After almost ten minutes of trying and failing to calm down, I sat up in the bed and called him. The phone rang a few times, then disconnected. I kept the phone against my ear with my eyes closed, not ready to deal with the possibility that he might've hung up when he saw my number. After a second the phone buzzed with an incoming text.

I was in my father's room. Walking outside to call you.

The relief that coursed through me was so intense, I sagged against the pillow with my phone clutched in my hand as I waited for the call. I picked up before the buzz turned into a ring.

"Hey." I sounded winded and was so tense I had to remind myself to blink.

There was a lot of noise wherever he was, but when he spoke I could hear the exhaustion in his voice. "I'm sorry I can't take you to Entoto today, but my father is not...well. My mom was afraid of leaving him alone, so I volunteered to stay so she and my sister could go home to rest."

This man did not need to be worrying about my feelings right now. "No, please don't apologize. I completely understand. How is he doing this morning?"

The long exhale on his end was almost answer enough. "His heart is fine, but they wanted to observe him overnight. He gets like this a lot,

130

terrified he's dying. He wasn't in a good headspace all night and this morning." He let out another long breath. "Wherever he is mentally, he's not feeling safe to go home at all, and I feel completely useless."

That sounded hard and complicated, and I didn't think it was my place to ask more. "I'm sorry," I said lamely.

"It is what it is." His voice was so flat and lifeless, such a contrast from yesterday.

"Is there anything I can do? Do you want me to bring something for you? Coffee or breakfast?"

"No." His tone was more forceful than I'd ever heard it. "My mother and sister will be here soon, and I'll go home."

"Oh, okay," I answered hesitantly, realizing his voice seemed almost panicked.

Of course, he was probably worried I'd show up and out him to his family. Because this wasn't a game, and even though Elias had been nothing but amazing and open over the past couple of days, this wasn't just a quick trip for him. This was his home, and his life had complications.

That eye-opener was the bucket of cold water I'd needed and hadn't gotten on my talk with Lucía. There were serious consequences to what we were doing, and I could just pack up and go home. Elias, on the other hand, could lose everything.

"I should probably let you go. Don't want to keep you from your dad. I hope you get some rest soon," I said, trying hard to sound normal, but failing miserably.

"Are you okay, Desta?" He was now worried about me, because my mess knew no bounds.

I tried really hard to inject some brightness in my voice. "Yes, of course. I hope your dad's on the mend soon. I'm glad you can be there with him."

Now he probably thought I was pissed at him, on top of the stress of what was going on with his dad. I needed to behave like an adult and not act out with someone who had enough to deal with.

"Take care of yourself too. You owe me a hike!" I congratulated myself on the little bit of cheerfulness I was able to manage, and the knot in my chest loosened somewhat when I heard Elias's laugh.

"Eshi, konjo. Have a good Sunday. We'll talk soon."

I ended the call feeling out of sorts and annoyed at myself. I wasn't in Ethiopia to pursue complicated relationships, no matter how amazing Elias was. I was here to think about my future and to get some closure around my father's death. Instead I'd been running around thirsting after a man who had hard enough decisions to make without me pushing myself into his life.

CHAPTER 17

It was 6:00 p.m. on a Sunday and I was sitting at my cubicle in the Aid USA office. After spending a good part of the morning exploring Piazza and the huge open-air market in Addis, I took a taxi up to the office, hoping to do some work while the place was empty. I wasn't surprised to find it half full of people with the same idea.

It was a common scene in the Aid USA offices I'd worked in. Expat life sometimes felt like summer camp. Balance could be elusive when personal and work lives melded this much. If I were honest, I'd been relieved to not have to spend the day in my own company. I ended up working on some of the adjustments to the surveys we'd need for the next round in the field, and even had time to send some emails out.

As I started packing up my stuff, I looked around and noticed a few others still around, including Bonnie and Sam. I was about to walk out when Bonnie came over and popped her head over my cubicle wall.

"We're good for tomorrow's trip. The data that came in from the first survey looks great, so thanks for that, both of you." She looked over at Sam, who was now standing and listening in on the conversation. "The way we ran the teams went so well, I think we should just go with that same strategy for this one."

I was tempted to ask if she had added a keeper for Sam in case he decided to harass any more government partners, but I refrained. He *had* been on his best behavior since we had to save his ass.

"Sam, you'll go with Nati, Solomon and Abe. Tsehay will be with her own team, and Desta, you can go with Elias and the two surveyors who rode with you before."

As soon as I heard Elias's name, my face felt hot. I cleared my throat, took a drink from my water bottle, and nodded without making eye contact. "Sounds good. Elias was great helping with the translation, and Abraham and Yohannes were awesome with the families. I'm excited for the next round!"

Down, boy.

Sam scoffed while putting away his stuff, but didn't say a word. I almost wished he would so I could tell Bonnie all the different ways we'd kept him from fucking up the project in the last couple of weeks. Thankfully, for once, he kept his mouth shut.

Bonnie raised an eyebrow, which read "what's with him," but I just shrugged, too annoyed to even get into it.

He smirked and looked at me with an expression that wasn't exactly friendly, but I could tell that he knew not to try me. "Desta and Elias work well together." He stretched out that last word like an ass, but when I narrowed my eyes he backed off quick. "Anyways, I'm headed home. Teams sound good."

That was as much of an olive branch as I was going to get from Sam, so I lifted my hand as he headed out and turned my focus back to Bonnie. "I'll see you a week from tomorrow, then? I'll connect with Elias tonight to make sure we're on the same page for our departure time."

She gave me a thumbs-up and seemed totally fine with me basically ignoring Sam. "Yes, I'll be there for the second week. We'll come up with a plan for the wrap-up then, before we cut you loose to go back to the U.S. of A."

It was like someone had punched me in the stomach. The thought of leaving and not seeing Elias again made me feel hollow inside. I gave Bonnie a forced smile as I tried once again to get myself together. "Oh, I'm in no rush to get back to DC."

That truth hit me hard. I didn't feel ready to face any of the things that were awaiting me when I got home. At the top of the list was the apartment with all of Miguel's stuff that he didn't bother taking with him. *So much baggage.* And here I was piling even more up with whatever I was doing with Elias. I felt weighed down with all of it.

"Are you okay, Desta?" Bonnie's worried voice broke me out of the chaos in my head and I did my best to come up with a smile.

"I'm good." She didn't seem to buy it, but I didn't think I could sound more convincing if I tried. "Must be hungry. I'm going to head out. Hopefully I'll find something open close to the guesthouse." I slid on my backpack and waved to Bonnie.

"Have a good night." She waved as I walked out of the room, her brows still furrowed from whatever she saw on my face.

I tried to shake off the funk I'd sunk into in the last few minutes as I walked out of the building, and remembered I told Bonnie I'd get in touch with Elias. Like I needed an excuse. I also wanted to know how his dad was doing, so I took out my phone and texted him.

Hey. How's your dad? Bonnie confirmed you'd be driving us down for this trip. Can't say I'm unhappy about that.

I stared at the phone for a few seconds and saw the three dots pop up as if he was typing a message, but then they disappeared. After another minute, no message came.

My heart sank. Disappointment made my limbs heavy. But what did I expect? Elias had a lot going on right now, and answering my needy texts was surely not at a priority. He was probably caring for his hospitalized father. I had to find something else to focus on, because Elias didn't need my drama.

I got myself together and walked to the parking lot with the plan of asking one of the guards to call me a cab. Just as I was headed to the security gate, I saw Bonnie getting into her car. She frantically waved me over, and when I attempted to walk past her and play dumb, she yelled at me, "Where are you off to looking so damn grumpy?"

I stopped and veered in her direction, feeling bad for ignoring her when she was just trying to be friendly. I could at least not be so fucking rude to someone who'd been nothing but nice to me. I jogged up to her car as she rolled down her window. "What are you up to tonight, Ms. Watts?"

She did have the most amazing laugh. "Getting the hell out of here before I get stuck doing more work for my boss. He's still in there." She jerked her thumb over at the building we'd just left. "That man thinks taking the weekend off is optional." That was said with an epic eye roll. "I'm about to meet some friends for dinner and drinks." She patted the passenger seat, then pointed at me. "You're welcome to come. Unless you've got other plans, of course."

I took my phone out and saw Elias had still not answered, then shoved it back in my pocket and gave her a nod. "Sounds great, actual-ly," I told her as I started moving toward the passenger side.

She leaned over to unlock the door for me. "Come on then! It's past six and there's a glass of wine with my name on it."

I jumped in, happy to have found a distraction, but I felt like an asshole too. I'd been so caught up with Elias, I'd made no effort to get to know Bonnie or anyone else from the office. It was about damn time I did.

Once we were on the road, she turned and gave me an assessing glance before returning her attention to the cluster of cars on the roundabout we were navigating. "Sam seems to have toned down his attitude." She sighed, but I kept my mouth shut. "I heard what happened with the woreda official and I reamed him out for it."

I wondered if she'd just invited me out to check-in about Sam's assholic behavior. "I'm sorry I didn't say anything."

She shook her head without looking at me, but she didn't seem too pissed. "He learned his lesson. And he's well aware y'all saved his ass."

"Sam, unfortunately, is not an anomaly in this line of work. On every job, there's always a Sam. I'm perfectly capable of putting him in his place." I thought of how Elias had to confront him. "What I don't like is how he treats some of our Ethiopian colleagues."

"Yeah, that I won't tolerate." She pursed her mouth at that as she drove through the city. When we passed the gigantic black Lion of Judah sculpture, she pointed at it. "Have you seen this yet?"

I leaned to get a closer look and shook my head. "No. I'd only seen it in pictures," I said, taking in the impressive monument, happy to change the subject.

"It was made in honor of the emperor's jubilee," she said with admiration.

I assumed she was talking about Haile Selassie, the last monarch of Ethiopia. "This place is sort of mind blowing."

She clicked her tongue at that. "It is, and hard to leave. I came here for a year and just closed in on a decade." We both laughed at that, but before I had time to talk, she went back to Sam. "Just so you know, I would never let him do or say anything that gets any of the local staff in trouble. We are guests here, and this work we do is a service. I believe that and expect every person who comes here to work to abide by it. I know Elias and Tsehay can stand up for themselves, but they shouldn't have to. If anything else happens out there, let me know. Okay?"

I nodded at how grave she looked. It was good to know that she took all of this seriously. "Thanks, Bonnie. I will." I sighed, looking out the window, my mind once again on Elias and wondering how he was doing.

"Elias is a great guy, you know? The best." The way she said that seemed far from casual, and I squirmed in my seat, wondering if people had been talking about the two of us.

"Umm, yeah, he is," I said cautiously, scrutinizing her face for any evidence that she was aware of what was going on with Elias and me, but she just kept driving in silence, wearing a neutral expression.

* * *

THE RESTAURANT WAS FANTASTIC. The owner had been an executive for one of those high-end burger franchises in the States and had come back to Addis Ababa to start her own business with a similar model. They had three kinds of burgers, fries, wine, and beer. Simple menu, but everything was delicious and had something of the local flavors mixed in.

I had a veggie burger topped with ayeb, a local cheese that resembled a chevre, with berbere fries, and loved it. I put another one in my mouth and moaned as Bonnie laughed at me. "Good, huh?"

"Oh my god, these are amazing. Tossing them in berbere is genius!" I was obsessed with the bright red thirteen-spice blend that was the base of Ethiopian cuisine. It was such a unique flavor, and apparently made everything delicious. The food and the company this evening had been great, and with my belly full of good food and two pints of St. George beer, I was feeling a lot more like myself.

I was sitting next to Brett, an Aussie who was in Addis working for Oxfam. I was half-listening to him tell a story about smuggling liters of vodka into Afghanistan in water bottles for some Marines who traded them for boxes of American cereal, butter and Ivory soap. So far the story was hilarious and involved various run-ins with camels. He kept looking at me and winking the more ridiculous the story got. I wasn't sure if I was up for flirting, but it felt nice to be here. Familiar. The expat scene was always sort of the same no matter where. It felt uncomplicated to be out with this group, and tonight that was a welcome feeling.

We stayed at the restaurant until almost 10:00 p.m., but eventually Bonnie and I begged off, explaining I had an early drive to the field. I got in the car with her after she said my guesthouse was on the way and she could drop me off.

We were laughing about the end of Brett's story—which involved carrying mac and cheese out of the Kabul embassy in condom boxes—when we pulled up to the guesthouse.

"He's so funny," I said. "And looks like I'm home. Thanks for letting me tag along. I had a great time."

"Oh, you're welcome. I was glad you came out. You'd been keeping to yourself. I was wondering if you were just not taking to Addis. I was happy to at least hear from Tsehay that you've been running with Elias in the mornings while you're in the field."

I immediately tensed at the second mention of Elias and me. I tried to figure out if I'd heard irony or suggestiveness in her tone, but she seemed to just be stating a fact.

"I've loved my time here so far." Elias's face immediately came to mind. And I knew then I would never be able to think about Ethiopia without thinking about him. "And I've been doing stuff. Yesterday I went to the pool at the Marquis with an old friend of my mom's."

It was dizzying to think it had only been a day since I'd been having dinner and flirting with Elias at Saba's house.

She clicked her tongue at that. "I forget you have a long history with this place," she said, looking at me closely as if trying to figure out if "my history" was getting to me.

I didn't need to get into how I'd fucked one of my co-workers, and if given the chance would totally do it again, so I settled for a something vague. "It's been good."

She waved me off, apparently satisfied I wasn't miserable, and I got out of the car with a promise to check in after we arrived at the site tomorrow.

I made myself wait until I was in my room to look at my phone for any messages from Elias. All night I'd been oscillating between telling myself not to give his silence so much weight to being convinced it was a sign I should give up this thing with him because his life was complicated enough already.

And really, what future could we possibly have?

Still, I told myself, we were friends. We could *stay* friends.

I checked as soon as I walked into my room, and my stomach dropped when I saw there were no messages on my phone. Immediately I started trying to convince myself it meant nothing. That he was probably scrambling to get ready for the long trip after dealing with a family emergency half the weekend. I'd get a report about his dad in person when I saw him tomorrow.

CHAPTER 18

I walked out into the cold pre-dawn Addis morning with an intense feeling of anticipation. After weeks of seeing Elias every day, yesterday had felt too long. And if I was honest, I needed the reassurance of seeing him after the stress of his dad's illness over the weekend. It was like I needed him to be physically there for things to be normal again.

As the white Land Cruiser pulled into the guesthouse, I waved happily at the driver, only to realize it wasn't him. I let my hand fall at my side, trying to not jump to conclusions.

Elias wouldn't leave me hanging without at least letting me know, right?

There were a lot of other international staff in this house who worked for Aid. It could be a driver picking up someone else. I knew Sam wasn't coming to the field until Wednesday, so it wouldn't be his driver. As I stared at the strange guy parking the car, my phone buzzed with a message. I pulled it out and saw there were a few texts from earlier in the morning.

I signaled to the driver to give me a second and tapped the screen of my phone. One message was from Bonnie, and the other three were all from Elias. The first one was from past midnight.

Sorry for the silence last night, konjo, my father declined after we brought him home yesterday. So we had to take him back to the hospital. When you texted me I was about to drive him there.

The second one was from 4:00 a.m. Had he gotten any sleep in the last two days?

I'm sorry, Desta. I won't be able to drive you today, I just can't leave my mom when things are so hectic. I hope to be able to come down midweek. Safe travels, konjo. Zebene will drive you and he's very good. Better than me!

The disappointment was so complete I actually stumbled as I walked to the car.

I quickly tapped out a message, thanking him for letting me know and telling him I hoped his father recovered quickly. But my fingers felt numb as the words I was typing appeared on the screen. I put my phone back in my pocket before throwing the bag in the back and coming up to the passenger seat. I climbed into the Land Cruiser with a big, fucked-up smile pasted on my face as Zebene started the truck.

He turned to me for a second as he maneuvered us out onto the street. "Good morning, Mr. Walker. I'm Zebene. Elias is taking some leave, so I will be driving you for the next few days."

I nodded in his direction with what I hoped was a friendly face. "Nice to meet you, Zebene. Please call me Desta, and Elias texted to let me know about the change. Thanks for coming to get me so early."

Zebene nodded and gave me a warm smile as he drove down the gravel path leading to the main road. "It's not a problem. Elias is a friend."

It looked like he wanted to say more, but instead he silently focused on the road. I wasn't going to ask if he knew more about Elias's dad since I wasn't exactly supposed to be aware of the goings-on of his personal life. I just made a friendly noise of acknowledgment and didn't say another word.

I was already wrung out from the roller coaster of feelings I'd been on this morning, and the sun wasn't even out yet. My skin felt tight from worry, but also because I was ashamed that Elias was going through so much and I had the nerve to feel sorry for myself. I needed to take things down a notch. More than that, I needed to let this go.

Zebene's voice mercifully yanked me out of my pity party, and I felt like an ass because I had no idea what he'd just said to me. "I'm sorry. You said something?"

He nodded, his eyes still on the road. "Just asking if you wanted to get breakfast and some bunna before we get on the road."

My stomach grumbled at the mention of food and coffee, and we both laughed. "Yes, please."

"Eshi. We can stop at Kaldi's."

My heart lurched at the mention of Kaldi's. Going there with Elias on that first morning felt like it happened a million years ago. Once again, I told myself I needed to concentrate on the work I was here to do and try to figure out what was next for *me*. As wonderful as things had been with Elias, I knew at some level I was using him as an excuse to not face the decisions I needed to make. I would take his absence as an opportunity to finally focus.

I pulled my sunglasses out of my bag and put them on as the sun rose, casting the city in an orange and purple glow. When I looked over at Zebene, I tried to project an ease I wasn't feeling just yet.

"Kaldi's sounds great."

CHAPTER 19

Once I got to the site, work started immediately. The second survey area we needed to cover was almost twice the size of the first one, in about the same time. I hit the ground running the moment I got there, and for the next few days had little time to think about Elias or my other self-made issues. I did make sure I texted him to ask about his dad, and he responded gratefully, letting me know he was doing much better. He also asked how things were going, and said he was looking forward to seeing me. I tried to be friendly and cordial, but also cut out all flirting from my texts to him.

Once it got into my head that chasing after Elias would only end in disaster for both of us, I'd forced myself to try to shut him out. It felt mean and shitty, but I was no longer able to do things halfway with him. If I let him in, he would be all the way back in, and *that* was madness.

So I kept my focus on my work and only turned the phone on at the end of the day to check if I had any messages from the Addis office. It had taken me a few weeks, but I'd finally gotten my head where it needed to be. I hated it, and hated that I missed him so much already, but I had brought this on myself. Lucía had been right—I did this, and I needed to stop.

On Wednesday evening as we pulled into the hotel, exhausted from almost ten hours of uninterrupted canvassing, I saw Elias standing by a white Land Cruiser talking to Tsehay. As soon as I saw him, my vision shrank to a tiny pinhole where only his face was visible. I closed my eyes, gripped the seatbelt strap with both hands, and took deep breaths. The need to go to him so strong I was lightheaded.

I worked on forcing myself not to jump out and throw myself at him—which would be very stupid in just about every way possible—as the truck came to a stop. So much for my "doing the right thing," since it only seemed to work when Elias was three hundred miles away.

A knock on the window startled me and I opened my eyes. I turned my head, still trying to get my breathing under control, and noticed Zebene was giving me a weird look. He probably thought I was carsick or something. I was about to tell him I was fine when my door opened and the now-familiar smell of Elias's cologne filled the space.

My belly fluttered, and that slightly nauseous feeling I got whenever he was near overtook me while I sat, hoping whatever I said didn't out us both. After giving me a radiant smile, he braced one arm on the frame of the door and stretched the other toward Zebene in greeting. They gripped each other's forearms in the manner I'd seen Ethiopian men do with each other as I sat there, mildly dizzy from Elias's proximity.

"Zebi, are you driving properly? Desta has very high standards!" Elias's jovial tone was only diminished by the weary look in his eyes.

Zebene laughed and looked over to me, presumably hoping for a response, except I had *nothing*. All my mental energy was occupied in trying not to be super obvious about how much I wanted to press my nose to Elias's neck, which at the moment was like, five inches from my face.

After a second he gave up and turned to Elias. "Desta finally knows what it's like to ride in a car with a real driver."

I did laugh at that, and used the distraction to get out of said vehicle before I lost it.

I spoke without looking at him. "Zebene has been great. It's good to see you, Elias. Can I get by?" I hated myself more with every word, but just as I asked, he stepped back and gave me space to get out. Once I was standing by the car, I turned to Zebene. "Thanks for everything. I'll see you in the morning?"

He shook his head and pointed at Elias. "Unfortunately, you will have to go back to withstanding the poor driving of my friend. I go back to Addis tomorrow."

Elias let out a laugh, but stopped after he got a good look at my face.

I kept my eyes focused on Zebene. This all felt so fucking wrong, but I didn't know what else to do. Elias and I couldn't be a couple. Hell, even being too familiar was inappropriate in like, ten different ways, not to mention potentially dangerous. "Have a good trip then. It's been great being out with you the past few days."

I turned to Elias before heading toward to my room. "How's your dad?"

"He's better now. Resting at home," he said cautiously, like he had no clue what to make of the way I was acting. And who could blame him?

"I'm glad he's better." And I really was, but I kept walking with my head down.

"How are you?" he asked as he followed me along the path that led to where I was staying. The hotel was more like a cluster of small cottages that were built to look like the traditional houses in the area, so they were scattered around the property. They were outfitted with all the necessary amenities: electricity, comfortable beds, hot water, and a lovely view of the mountains. It was sort of like glamping, and my cottage was at the far end of the property.

"Desta?"

I stopped as I got to my door, still not ready to answer his question. The simple *yes* that should've immediately come out of my mouth was stuck in my throat, and I knew that what would spill out was certainly not the way to go.

"Konjo?" He said it quietly, barely a whisper, and the endearment managed to seriously weaken my defenses. Then I remembered this was nothing but a convenient distraction for me, and a potentially huge problem for him.

I finally looked at him and saw his furrowed brow, the darkness under his eyes. He hadn't been sleeping. He looked tired. And here I was feeling sorry for myself. Making this all about me. The least I could do was give him an answer.

"I'm all right. Tired from the long days. It's good to see you, Elias." Hadn't I said that already? I'd made such a fucking mess of things.

"Elias…" My eyes darted away from him. "I've been thinking, and I just don't know if this"—I waved a hand in front of the two of us, looking at a spot somewhere over his shoulder—"is a good idea."

I felt him straighten, and when he spoke, he was dead serious. "Did I do or say anything to make you uncomfortable?"

Fuck, I should've known I'd worry him. "No, not at all. It's just that you have a lot going on with your dad, and I'm just a leech sucking up your time and energy. You don't need to be dealing with me on top of everything."

I looked down and saw his hands flexing, opening and closing, like he was itching to grab me. A swarm of bees buzzed in my chest, wanting him to reach for me. Hoping he'd stop this and we could go back to the way it had been just a few days before.

But he didn't do that. He considered me for a moment before speaking with that same careful manner he always had. "I have not been 'dealing' with you." I could hear the air quotes in the word. "I've been getting to know you. Desta, you don't have to be my protector. It may be hard for you to believe, but I'm perfectly capable of deciding which things and which people I want to spend my time with. You don't know better than I do about what I can take on."

I flinched, remembering what he'd shared about his ex. But this was just one more way in which this was all just a bad idea.

"I'm very tired, Elias." I lifted a shoulder, feigning an exhaustion that had evaporated the moment I'd set eyes on him. "Long day. I'll just have some dinner in my room and turn in early," I said, making a show of yawning.

His face, which had been open when he'd first seen me, was now shuttered and unhappy. His full lips pursed as he gave me a terse nod. "If you're tired and you are done with me, I won't push you, Desta. But don't use me as an excuse to punish yourself. I don't play those games."

I hated being the one putting an unhappy expression on that mouth, which was made for smiling. I hated that I'd ruined everything. I wanted to tell him to forget what I'd said. To ask him into my room, and kiss him. Touch him until he made everything right again.

But I didn't. "I'm sorry."

He backed away, and before turning up the path, he looked up, a stricken expression on his face. "I hope you get some rest, then. We leave at 7 a.m."

* * *

THE NEXT DAY WAS...THE worst. Elias was clearly uncomfortable, and I tried to overcompensate by being too enthusiastic about everything. By the time we were headed back to the hotel, I was mentally wrung out and so jumpy I had to grip the edge of my seat to keep from yelping any time we hit a dip in the road. Yohannes and Abraham had asked us to drop them off in the center of town so they could do some shopping, leaving Elias and me alone in the Cruiser. I looked at him as he drove, his face stark and unhappy. He'd been giving bemused looks all day, and barely spoke to me as we drove through the villages we were surveying.

I couldn't blame him for looking confused. I hardly knew what I was doing, and kept behaving like an asshole. He'd told me he would back off, gave me what I wanted, and that only made me even more miserable. Every cordial word he directed my way, every respectful question put me on edge, but now that I'd started this I didn't know how to take it all back. And what was more, I still thought it was for the best, no matter how fucked-up it made me feel.

I took a deep breath as we drove and decided I was going to make conversation like a fucking human being, because I was sick of this shit. "Saba asked me to tell you she wants to get your opinion about her new project."

He gave me a startled look, his eyes widening in disbelief. "Really?"

"Yes, really. I'll send you her number. That way you can contact her directly."

"Thank you." He looked over at me, his handsome face tense, but didn't say more.

I scrambled for other things to talk about, trying to ward off the awkward silences that kept sucking the oxygen from the space between us. "Did you get a chance to rest before you had to drive down here?"

He shrugged but kept looking at the road. "Yes. The last day I was there, my dad was better and my mom was home, so I slept. It was nice having time at home with her. Family's hard sometimes, but they're my people." He sighed then, and it sounded so heavy. I wasn't sure what he was going to say, but when he did speak it was like he was talking to my soul. "It's hard to know sometimes where their expectations end, and my own happiness begins."

I looked at his profile. He seemed so worried, so exhausted. I was tempted to just mouth off some platitude to make him feel better, but tried for honesty instead. I at least owed him that.

"My mom was so fragile after my dad died. I stayed in Ithaca for college because I couldn't put her go through losing me too. After I graduated, I let her push me to work in humanitarian relief. She thought it would be a great way to honor my dad, and in some ways I did too."

I bit my lip, mortified at voicing something I'd hardly let myself think about. "Like by doing the same work he did, I'd feel closer to him somehow. I never even considered another career." I lifted a shoulder, feigning levity I didn't feel. "It's so funny because my dad was a free spirit, man. He did whatever the fuck he wanted. I don't think he'd be very impressed with me."

Elias shook his head, seemingly unhappy with my comment. This time he did turn to look at me, his eyes serious. "Don't say that. You're a good man, Desta. Brave."

I wanted to scoff or dismiss his words, but I let him finish.

"It's not an easy thing to turn your back on the dreams the people you love have for you. Sometimes the hardest choices are between living for yourself and fulfilling the hopes they have for you."

He paused, and after a moment spoke in a voice filled with ache. "There have been many times when I've asked myself if seeing pride light up my mother's eyes is more important than letting her know who I really am." His face looked so grim in that moment, resigned. "It hurts to know it's only a matter of time before I put it out, but I'm so tired of hiding."

I didn't know what to say. This was not where I thought the conversation would go and I was feeling completely out of my depth. Elias was not out to his mother—the secret was hurting him. But I also didn't want to be the reason he rushed this or made any rash decisions. I wasn't sure I was worth it.

I turned my face to look out the window, trying to think how to answer. "None of these things are easy, Elias. Why do we have to be responsible for the light in anyone's eyes? Is it even fair to put that burden on us?" I pressed my cheek to the glass and closed my eyes. "It all makes me so tired, you know?"

After a moment, I felt his hand squeeze mine for a second. I stiffened but didn't pull away. If he noticed, he didn't say.

CHAPTER 20

The rest of the week flew by. The new survey area was not as populated as the first one, so we had to travel long distances between sites, which meant a lot of time in the car. I spent hours talking with Abraham and Yohannes, with Elias's help. I asked how they thought the families were answering questions, or what else we could do to make them more responsive or at ease.

Elias was extremely efficient in keeping the communication flowing, but after a couple of days he had completely stopped any attempts at more private conversations with me. He was polite and professional, but he kept his distance. No konjo, no runs, nothing. Which was exactly what I wanted.

I should have been happy with things as they were. Except I was miserable and wished I could take it all back. But I'd be damned if I was going to be one of those people who played out their insecurities at the expense of others. I had gone down this road because I knew in the end it was for the best, and I would see it through.

Meanwhile, I was getting increasingly annoyed at myself for noticing every move that Elias made, every word he exchanged with someone. It was so fucking unhealthy. I tracked him as he walked around the villages, laughing with the families we visited, picking up their kids, chasing them around. He was so good with everyone, and I desperately missed being the focus of his attention.

I wasn't happy unless I was grasping at straws, and Elias had become my new way to punish myself.

That night when we pulled up to the hotel, I practically jumped out of the car the moment it stopped moving. As I grabbed my backpack, I looked at Elias. "See you at dinner."

I expected him to nod and drive off, but instead he rubbed the back of his neck and said, "I won't be at dinner tonight. See you in the morning."

I managed to respond, and I was fairly certain my tone disguised the fact that my chest caved into my spine. "Sure, no problem. Have a good night."

He said goodbye and turned the truck around to take it to the parking lot in the back of the property. I walked back to my room, doing everything I could to avoid thinking about how I was feeling.

I showered and changed, then came down to the dining room where there were already a few people from our group talking and drinking beers. Sam was there with Tsehay, Abraham, and one of the drivers. For once he didn't seem like he was berating them or acting like an asshole, but I still didn't feel like dealing with him.

I didn't feel like dealing with anyone.

I almost turned around and went back to my cottage, but sulking because Elias decided to pass up on another chance to be ignored by me would be next-level messy.

I walked over to the bar and ordered a beer, wanting to have a few minutes to myself before I joined the others at the table. Tsehay gestured at a chair between her and Abraham, but I held my hand up, letting her know I needed a moment.

I looked around the room as I sipped my beer. The dining room was its own building, designed in the same traditional style as the cabins. From the outside it looked like they had pushed three enormous beehives together. Inside it was long and wide, and smelled like the wood they used to make it. There were large windows running along the walls, and we could see the lamps lighting the paths to the rooms. They were open right now, and there were all kinds of sounds coming in.

The night was always buzzing with critters and animals serenading our evening meals. Crickets, cicadas, and the occasional hyena made for quite the symphony. Later, when everyone had gone to bed, packs of hyenas would start circling the property and would whoop all night. It was creepy as fuck, and when Elias first told me about it, I joked he'd have to sneak into my room and protect me while we were staying here. He just laughed and told me he'd buy me a flashlight.

I had it in my pocket right now, actually. The morning after he arrived I found a little red flashlight sitting on the passenger seat of the Cruiser, because even though I'd been acting like a complete asshole, he was still kind and kept his promises.

Remembering how easy things had been with us just a week ago and how shitty they felt now sank my mood even further. In an attempt to drag myself out of my funk, I tuned back into what was happening around me and focused my attention on the Ethiopian music coming in through the speakers. The woman's voice was so melancholy, like her heart was breaking, and a guitar or some other string instrument was blending with her words, making it the perfect sorrowful companion. I closed my eyes to listen. Her singing was so beautiful I could have cried.

When it ended I opened my eyes and turned to see Tsehay standing next to me.

"That was beautiful and sounded really sad," I told her.

She squeezed my shoulder, obviously catching on to my mood. "Ethiopia has gotten under your skin, Desta." I almost laughed, because if she only knew how much. "That was Aster Aweke." Tsehay explained and I nodded, recognizing the name of the popular pop singer. "She was singing Tizita—it's like our version of the blues." She smiled sadly at that, and I remembered how soulful her voice was. I wondered where that depth came from. "Tizita means something like a memory with a tinge of regret."

I shook my head and laughed a humorlessly. "Figures."

"I sing this one sometimes when we play at Black Orchid."

I smiled at her casual mention of her alter ego and changed the subject, desperate to get off my moping. "That's right, we haven't had a chance to talk about your star power."

She gave me a smirk, but her face did not look amused. She sat by me and then quietly asked, "Where's Elias?"

Okay, so she was on to me.

I schooled my face in a neutral expression and answered, "Not sure. He said he was going to skip dinner."

She kept her eyes on me for another moment without speaking. I panicked. Because if Tsehay suspected something, that meant other people might too. She took pity on me and whispered, "I know."

Before I had any time to react, her voice dropped even lower, and she looked up to the table where our group was chatting a few yards away. "I was the one who introduced Eli to his ex." She grimaced. "Which was a big mistake. He hasn't said anything about you guys, but I know him. We've been friends since university."

I was too shocked to have any clever replies, so I took another gulp of my beer and sat there in silence. She chuckled at whatever expression I was making. "He seems happy, and maybe this thing with you will give him the push he needs to finally be a little selfish, and take his chance."

I shook my head, unsure of what she was implying. "You mean going to the States."

"Yes, he's been agonizing about that for over a year. The issues with his father and then the disappointment with Byron have held him back. But he needs to go. Eventually the hiding and the secrecy are going to get to him, and that would be a shame."

The weariness in her voice made me think she was speaking from experience. I wasn't even sure what to say, but she was waiting for an answer, so I made myself say something.

With my eyes trained in the direction of the group, I spoke honestly. "I'm not sure I'm worth Elias potentially ruining his relationship with his parents." I glanced at Tsehay, scowling as if she did not see eye to eye with me on that at all.

"I think that decision is not completely up to you." Her expression softened then. "And I don't think it would be all about you—he needs to do this at some point. Hiding like that, it eats at you. It will wear him out eventually. He needs to breathe freely for a while, at least to know what it's like. He can't keep using his family as an excuse not to do that."

She sighed, as if wondering if the emotional toil of going on with this conversation was worth it. But then she moved closer, her eyes half-closed. "There is so much going on in our country. So many vital things to focus on, work toward…it's hard to prioritize things that don't seem essential. But we must do that too. It's not being frivolous to think about our own happiness, our safety in here." She tapped a finger to her temple and then somewhere by her heart. "How can we do this work we do if we are walking around with big holes in our chests?"

My eyes widened at the *we*. Her closeness with Elias made total sense now. She must have figured out my curiosity because she smiled as she cocked her head in the direction of the table. "I'll tell you my story some time, Desta. Come on, let's join the table before Sam decides we're sleeping together."

I rolled my eyes and as I finished my beer before glancing over at him. "He's such an ass."

Tsehay didn't answer, but she didn't have to. After a moment, we moved to join the others. All through dinner I thought about what she'd told me and decided I needed to talk with Elias. Even if we couldn't be together, he deserved better than what he was getting from me.

* * *

THE NEXT MORNING I was out of my room and headed for a run just as the sun was coming up. I had my headphones on and set out on my usual route. I had actually gotten used to the weird whooping sounds the hyenas made and had a decent night of sleep. My body was eager for some exercise, and as soon as I set out, I felt awake and energized.

I ran alongside the two-lane road, which went up rolling hills. On either side of me were rows and rows of coffee bushes still half hidden in the morning mist. There were traditional houses interspersed with the orchards a bit farther in from the road. In the distance I saw green mountains looming.

It was so beautiful here.

My mom had been right—there *was* just something in the air. After over a month, my heart felt bigger. Like coming back to this place was a puzzle piece I'd been missing.

As I ran and the sun settled higher in the sky, I started to notice the now-familiar smells of the mornings. Smoke from wood fires were burning, boiling water to make the morning's breakfast and tea or coffee.

I let my mind go and focused on what I knew already. I liked this work, but I wanted to do more at home. I wanted to work with LGBTQ+ youth. Children of immigrants and refugees who were trying to navigate life in the States and were probably struggling to blend those identities of who they were to their families and who they were inside. The only issue was telling my mother. Well, that and Elias, what I felt for him. Which by now I knew was not something that would just go away, and I still had no idea what to do about it. And I was scared of hurting my mom by taking the last tangible thing she had that connected her to my dad.

But I couldn't keep that going at my own expense. Like I'd told Elias, it wasn't fair to have all that on my shoulders. I had to do it. The mere thought of working in something different and closer to home made me feel lighter, and for the first time in days, I felt like I could take in a deep breath.

By the time I was about half a mile back to the hotel, the sun was up and I had my usual entourage of boys from the village running after me. I sprinted as far as I could for the last couple of hundred yards and doled out the stash of hard candy I had in my hoodie pocket to those who kept up to the end.

I stumbled into the courtyard and was doing some stretches before I noticed Elias had just run in as well. "Hey, I didn't see you out there."

He startled when he saw me and started moving toward the room, giving me a wide berth. "I went another way, a longer trail. We leave in an hour."

Not a smile, not a wave. Nothing. He just left me standing there, and I completely deserved it.

CHAPTER 21

That afternoon we were getting in the car at the end of the day when Elias turned to me and asked, "Would you mind if we stop by one the houses we visited earlier this week? They're just about twenty minutes out of the way. I want to drop something off."

At this point I was so desperate to get any sort of approval from him that I automatically nodded. "Sure, no problem. Did we forget something there?"

"No, I have something for them."

"Okay." That was a pretty cryptic answer, but he didn't seem like he was going to offer more information, so I just put my head back and closed my eyes for the ride.

I must have dozed off, because I came to when Elias slammed the door on his side. He popped his head through the car window and said, "I'll be right back."

I twisted around to spy on what he was doing and saw him run to the back of the vehicle and take two black plastic bags out. He quickly walked up a stone path that led to a set of three houses clustered together on a little hill. Each one had a garden in front, which this time of year had lots of veggies hanging from well-cared for plants.

When he got to the one in the center, he looked inside the house, but waited outside.

After a moment a woman and two girls came out. I remembered them from the survey. They'd been curious when we were in their home, shyly asking questions. Elias greeted the mom and smiled at the girls as he handed them the bags. The woman's face lit up and the little girls started peeking in. Soon another woman from a neighboring house came over with her girl as well. The mom from the first one started riffling through the bags, hefting out a pile of notebooks and school supplies, then passed it to her neighbor.

The woman threw her hands up and bowed to Elias, who shook his head like it was too much. He spoke to them for a couple of minutes as the girls got out the stuff he brought and the women nodded vehemently at whatever he was saying. Not long after, they said their goodbyes, and Elias jogged back to the truck and started us back toward the main road. Abraham and Yohannes spoke up from the back in Amharic, their voices amused.

After a moment I turned to him. "So you got some notebooks for the kids? That's nice."

He looked at me for a moment as if trying to figure out what my curiosity meant, but he just answered my question. "When we were here, I was talking to the mothers and they asked if I knew of any program that had school supplies for girls. You know how hard it can be for girls to go to school, especially in the rural areas, but these women want their girls to attend. They saved up to buy them the uniforms, which, when you have as little as they do, can mean sacrificing other things. But they didn't have the notebooks and other supplies, so I thought I'd bring them some to encourage them." He shrugged like it was no big deal.

"Is that what you did last night after we got back?"

"Yes, I went to the stationery store in town, since we'd be out before they opened this morning. We're going to another area next week, so I wanted to bring them these while we were not too out of the way."

I didn't deserve him. He was entirely too pure and too good.

While I'd spent my week freezing him out, letting my insecurities and baggage come between us, he was going about life the way he always did, using his time and energy to do what was right. To stop and notice what was needed and trying to make a difference.

I felt ashamed at how I'd behaved toward him in the last few days. How I'd decided for Elias that coming out to his family was something he was not strong enough to do. What made it worse was that I knew none of this was about him. No. This was about me. My fear that once someone decided I was worth fighting for, I would have to live up to it.

Elias kept driving in silence, and after a while turned to me. "Will you play something for us?" His face looked so sad. Like he could see all my fucked-up feelings and insecurities. I needed to talk to Elias, let him know why I had acted the way I did. I could've said something then, apologized or at least hinted at the fact that I knew I'd been wrong. But I chickened out.

"I'll put something on," I said grabbing my iPhone. I scrolled through the music until I found a blues playlist I'd downloaded for him. I hit play, and the unmistakable notes of "Mannish Boy" by Muddy Waters broke through the humming of the truck.

Then something happened that felt like seeing the sun come out after days of rain: he smiled at me. The first real smile I'd seen in what felt like weeks. "This is perfect. Thank you."

I nodded and smiled back as we both settled in with the music and rode home. And when the gravelly coming through the speakers told us everything would be all right, I almost believed it.

* * *

It was dark by the time we got back to the lodge. As soon as we parked, Elias jumped out and started unloading the truck. I went around to ask if he needed help, but he waved me off.

"There are just a few things. I'll be done in a minute. Go shower."

I hesitated, unsure if it was the right time to say something, but decided to oblige him. I walked into the main lodge, hoping to get a few bottles of water for my room. I was surprised to find Bonnie by the front desk. We weren't expecting her for a couple more days, and by the looks of it, neither was the lodge. Her face was a study in resignation when I walked up to her, but she lit up once she saw me.

"Hey! How's it going? I hope my arrival isn't an issue. I can just ride along on whatever you're doing for the next couple of days. If I can get a room to sleep in, that is!"

I waved her off, genuinely happy to see her. "Of course it's not an issue. Glad to have you with us. Is there a problem with your room?"

She looked over her shoulder at the disgruntled front desk clerk, then back at me. She was decked out in one of her many tunic and jeans combos, but this time she was wearing heavy-duty hiking boots instead of Birkens, her white hair in its usual messy topknot.

She spared another look for the man at the front desk, who was tapping helplessly on the keyboard. "I knew it would be ill-advised to head down here early, but I figured they could make it work for a couple of nights. Unfortunately, it seems they're not only full for the next few days, but they double-booked the room I was supposed to have when I arrived on Sunday. They won't have a room for me until Wednesday."

"Is there another place in town you could go until then?"

She made me a face at my question. "Oh no, this is not my first rodeo." With that she turned back to the front desk, obviously ready for another round. I was about to offer to share my room, I only had one bed though. It wasn't a big deal for me, but I knew Bonnie needed her space.

She was in a heated discussion with the clerk when I put my hand on her shoulder, interrupting the exchange. "Hey Bonnie, why don't you just take my room? I can ask one of the other guys if I can crash with them. No big."

The thought of having to room with Sam made a shiver of apprehension run down my spine, but I was willing to suffer for a few days.

Bonnie perked up at my suggestion and glanced at the clerk, who was looking at me like I had just rescued a small village. "Are you sure? Because I'll take it. I'm not gonna do the 'Oh, you shouldn't, I don't want to put you out' bullshit. I will take the damn room and leave you to your own devices."

I really liked this woman. "Yes, I'm sure," I said with a laugh.

At that moment Elias walked in. Bonnie's face lit up and she greeted him with the Ethiopian double kiss and double embrace. "As always, Elias, you're right on time. I did it again!" She threw her hands in the air while Elias grinned at her antics. "I decided to come early, and now I don't have a place to sleep."

He smiled at her with affection while she waved her hand in my direction.

"Thankfully, Desta here has gallantly offered me his room. I, of course, accepted before he could take it back, but now he's roomless. Can he bunk with you? I think you got one of the doubles when we reserved, right? It'll be tight, but—"

Before she could finish, Elias shrugged and said with the most nonchalant face I had ever seen, "Sure." Then he turned to me and asked, "Is it fine for you, Desta?"

I swallowed hard, twice. I nodded, trying not to let my panic show as I walked to the door of the lodge. The only thing that came out of my mouth was, "I'll get my stuff."

CHAPTER 22

I walked into Elias's room and immediately noticed it had one big bed with a smaller cot to the side. At least it appeared like two people could sleep here. I looked back at him as he leaned against the door, his arms crossed in front of his chest, but he was not offering any conversation at the moment.

The room was…small. I knew Abraham, Yohannes, and some of the other staff had decided to stay in cheaper lodgings so they could save some of their per diem. Elias had opted to stay here, though. Now I wondered if he'd done it to be closer to me, just to have me act like a brat toward him all week.

We stood there, unable to bridge the distance my actions had put between us. I hated myself for starting this. After I put down my bag by the bathroom door, I turned and tried to school my face into a friendly expression. "So! This is awkward."

He didn't even crack a smile. He moved to the bigger bed, sat on the edge, and said in a distant but clear tone, "I can go into town and get a room there. I don't want to make you uncomfortable."

His voice completely lacked inflection, like he'd stripped all emotion from anything he had to say to me. He didn't look hurt. He didn't even look angry. He was simply indifferent, and that was *so* much worse.

"I'm not uncomfortable with you. I know I've been a little distant this week—"

He scoffed as if saying *understatement of the year*, and I couldn't blame him. I had done a complete one-eighty on him. Had changed my mind so fast I had given *myself* whiplash.

I sighed and sat on the floor in front of his spot on the bed. "This is so stupid, Elias. I'm sorry I've been such an asshole this week. Now that I'm here sitting with you after this afternoon, when I once again saw the kind of man you obviously are, I feel so frivolous and ridiculous for shutting you out because of my own insecurities."

He was looking at me like I baffled him, and right now, not at all in a good way. "Desta, I don't understand what happened. One moment things were going so well, and the next you acted like I was a stranger. If I did something to offend you—or worse, hurt you—I'm sorry. But the way you treated me? I didn't deserve that."

My face burned from humiliation. He was right. He hadn't deserved that. For all that I agonized about not wanting to put my baggage on other people, I'd done just that, and during a time when he'd needed me to be a friend.

I opened my mouth to say I was sorry, but instead I overshared.

"I didn't want to add to what you were already dealing with. Your dad is sick, and you've got all kinds of decisions to make." I lifted my hands up, not sure where I was going with my rambling. "And then there's the fact that it's not even safe for you to be doing this. I didn't want to make your life harder."

He exhaled and grabbed at his curls the way I'd seen him do whenever a conversation got intense. "So instead of telling me that, you shut me out and took away my choices? You don't have to save me from myself or otherwise, Desta."

With every word out of this mouth, I felt more and more ashamed of how I'd acted. He looked up at the pointed ceiling of the cottage and took a long breath before he continued. "You know what hurt the most about Byron?"

I shook my head, but he was still looking up. "It wasn't the ugly things he said. It was that he thought he knew better than me. That he believed I couldn't decide on my own what I did and didn't want." He lowered his eyes to me then, and I felt sorry for putting the hurt in them. "You don't think I know the risks? That this has never come up for me?"

"Of course you do."

The laugh he let out was brittle and jaded, and I wanted the earth to swallow me up. "I know exactly what it meant to reach for you. To make love to you. The risks I was taking. But I took them anyway because I wanted you. Because I thought you could see me and want me without turning me into something you had to save."

That cut the deepest because I deserved it.

"I'm so fucking sorry, Elias." It seemed like such a trite thing to say. "That sounds so stupid."

He closed his eyes for a moment, gathering his thoughts. Figuring out what to say. How to say it. "Since I've been with you, I've begun to wonder how much longer I can go on keeping all these secrets. You've made think very hard about how I want to live from now on." He sighed. "I had news to tell you when I arrived from Addis. When you barely spoke to me, it hurt."

I was such an ass. "Elias, I don't even know what to say."

"You don't have to keep apologizing." He still held his body uncomfortably, as if he didn't want to get too close. "I want to know that you see me as your equal."

"Of course I see you like that," I protested.

"Then give me the chance to decide for myself what I can and cannot have."

We stayed there for a minute, not saying anything. He'd had good news to share with me and my behavior had ruined it for him. I leaned closer and looked at him, hoping he could see how terrible I felt. "Is it too late to tell me now?"

He let out a long breath and ran his hand through his hair, pulling on the ends again. "I've contacted Columbia to confirm my attendance this fall."

I snapped my head up, unable to hide huge the smile that broke on my face. "You decided? What changed?"

He lifted a shoulder. "It's too big of an opportunity to pass up."

I wasn't disappointed when he didn't say I'd been part of the reason. I wasn't that delusional. But I was sad I'd tainted the moment for both of us.

"It's an amazing opportunity." I meant it, and my head filled with the possibilities of what it could mean for both of us.

"I don't know if I could live with myself if I didn't go. But it's scary, because I know if I leave, it may be for good." The agony in his face was complete. "I want so very much to be strong enough to come back and work on changing the things that need changing, but I'm feeling selfish."

He shook his head hard, his tight curls swaying with the force of his movements. "It's unfair that I have to choose between living openly as a gay man and living in my country. Because before anything else, I *am* Ethiopian. This place, this land is at the core of who I am, and it pains me to admit my relief when I thought about not having to hide anymore."

I was disgusted with myself for having made an already terrible situation for Elias even worse. I was also feeling for him. Though I could never fully understand his situation, I could empathize with the struggle of choosing himself over something he loved.

I got on my knees and took his hand. "Elias," I said, my voice hoarse with emotion. "I'm sorry this decision has to be so hard for you. You're right. It isn't fair, but you never know—maybe with time and distance you'll be in a better position to change things. You should be so proud of yourself. It's a huge accomplishment."

He was starting to smile, his hand tightly holding mine. I was desperate to relieve the tension of the last few minutes, so I went with something I knew would at least amuse him. "Betam Gobez."

Elias chuckled at my horrible attempt at telling him he was clever in Amharic. I looked down, trying not to make too much of the change in the mood. Trying not to ruin it by doing something that was unwelcome.

Then I felt Elias's fingers caress the side of my face. I pushed into his touch, almost ready to sob from the contact. I missed his hands on me. His warmth. The way he was firm and gentle at the same time. Elias's touch made everything so much simpler.

"Elias," I said, breathlessly as our eyes locked.

"Can I kiss you, konjo?"

I didn't answer, just stood and climbed onto his lap. He immediately grabbed me roughly.

"Desta." My name coming out of his mouth sounded like a prayer. "I've missed you."

"I've missed you too." I pushed my body against his, holding his face between my hands before going in for a kiss. Our tongues tangled together, bodies pressed tightly. I rocked my hips against him, and I could feel him harden. I reveled at being able to touch him like this. To run my hands over his warm skin. To feel him react to me.

I shuddered out a breath as I pulled back for some air. Elias's fingers were digging into my flesh like he never wanted to let me go. I laid my head on his shoulder, pressing my lips to his neck. "I'm sorry I pushed you away."

He shook his head as he moved us, dislodging me from his lap for a moment so we could move farther up the bed. He sat with his back to the headboard and I climbed right back on his lap, huffing as I got comfortable again. "This is where I want to be."

He laughed, but then his face got serious again. "Konjo, next time you're feeling like you want some distance, please tell me what you're thinking first. At least give me the chance to decide for myself."

I nodded, rattled by how scared I'd been when I thought I'd done something unforgivable. Elias had made such a huge decision this week: he was going to leave his country, the people he loved, and everything he knew, in the hope of finding a place where he could be himself. "You're so brave. I wish I could be that strong."

He squeezed me tight as I spoke. "You *are* brave. Look at what you've done, the work you do all over the world. Going to places so far away without hesitation and doing hard things. Coming here because it was important to your father and your mother. All those things are brave."

I shrugged off his compliments. "It doesn't feel brave. It feels like hiding. The longer I avoid telling my mother I don't want to do this work anymore, the longer I avoid dealing with the possibility that maybe social work in the States won't fulfill me either. That I'm not suited for any of this."

Elias leaned back so he could look at me. "I've been working for Aid USA for almost five years and I've seen dozens of international consultants come through here. None of them have been as respectful and thoughtful in doing their work as you. All the local staff have mentioned how much they've liked working with you."

My chest warmed at his words and the sincerity with which he said them. "Thank you for that."

"You're welcome, but it's the truth."

We held each other for a while longer, and I looked at him again. "Is your dad really doing better?" Since the chat with Tsehay the other night, I'd wondered if there was more going on that I didn't know.

The way Elias brought me closer to him before he spoke told me I was right. "My dad has severe anxiety. It's always been manageable—with its ups and downs, of course—but his heart condition in recent years has really exacerbated it. When he's very stressed, he starts feeling ill, and then becomes terrified he's dying. We take him to the hospital so he can get checked out."

I took one of the hands he'd fastened across my chest and held it. "That can't be easy for any of you."

He lifted a shoulder, his face resigned. "There's a lot of stigma around mental illness here, so he won't even consider getting help for any of it." He smiled, but it did not reach his eyes. "The ironic part is that it's my profession, you know? I could help him get some care, but he says people will think he's crazy or weak."

I nodded sadly. "I can't imagine how hard it is for you to see your dad suffer like that," I said, looking up at his face, which had been happy a minute ago and now was marred with worry. "Things are changing in the States, but there is still a lot to do when it comes to mental illness. It's not taken nearly as seriously as it should be. Society acts like it's just something people should be able to 'get over.' It's fucking ridiculous."

Elias exhaled, and I could feel the tension in his shoulders. "It's affected my family a lot. My dad is a pianist, but he stopped working or making music when I was in elementary school. Said he couldn't do it anymore." He shrugged, but I could tell how all this weighed on him. "My mom supported the family, for the most part. It's too hard for him to stay in a job, so he feels useless because he doesn't contribute financially to the home, though none of us care about that. He took great care of us growing up while my mom worked, but it's hard for him to see that."

I listened to him as I ran my hands up and down his thighs, which were on either side of mine, wanting to ease what was clearly painful for him. "I imagine there's also the issue of the expectation for him to go to work and provide for the family."

Elias nodded, holding me tighter. "Exactly. He always says he's grateful for my mom, but I think he also resents the situation. When he's really low, he becomes obsessed with the idea that he's dying, and my mom either believes it or goes along with it to appease him. It's a vicious cycle." He gave a tired sigh. "That's part of the reason why I deferred from Columbia. I didn't want to leave her to deal with it on her own. My sister was living in Kenya for a few years and just came back. With her around, my mom has more support, and I can go to New York."

That explained so much. I wanted to say more to ease his mind, but I had no idea what, if anything, could help. Still, I had to say something. "I know it may not be of much comfort now, but I think you made the right decision. This *is* too big of a chance to pass up, and you've earned it."

He looked a bit unsure, but he bent his head to kiss me anyway. After a moment, he jumped as if something had startled him, then lifted his arm to look at his watch. "We have to hurry, or we will miss dinner with the group."

I tightened my arms around his neck and groaned. "I don't want to move, and I *really* don't want to go listen to Sam droning on about how amazing he is."

Elias laughed and squeezed me hard. "I know, but now that we're roommates, the faster we get done with dinner, the faster we can come back, and I can show you how Ethiopians make up."

That perked me up fast, and soon I was out of the bed and rifling through my bag for my shaving kit.

Elias just looked at me, amused. "Finally, Bonnie's utter inability to make a proper reservation has reaped some benefits."

CHAPTER 23

Once Elias and I sorted things out, it was like a fog had been lifted. We worked hard on that second survey, taking only a couple of days off the entire time. During the day we crisscrossed southern Ethiopia gathering data, and in the evenings, Elias and I slept in each other's arms as if we'd been doing it for years. Now we were on our way back to Addis, and my time in Ethiopia felt like it was slipping through my fingers.

After almost two months I was down to my last ten days, which I would use to work on cleaning up the data we'd gathered, and then I was taking some time to travel around. We'd discussed Elias coming with me, but he had a lot to work out for his departure to the States, which included coming out to his family. He didn't have much time to do it, either. His advisor at Columbia had requested he arrive early so he could assist with a seminar over the summer. Elias had to be in New York City in six weeks at the latest.

As for me, I still had no idea what I was going to do. We hadn't talked about it explicitly, but given the conversations of the past few weeks, it was clear that we were both focusing on our separate plans and not wanting to write anything in stone when it came to us. It wasn't for lack of wanting, though. I was itching to say reckless shit, tell him I loved him, that even if I ended up going back to DC, I still wanted to try to be together, but I didn't want to muddy the already-complicated waters of his departure with my neediness.

"Konjo." Elias's soft voice brought me out of my thoughts, and I looked out the window to realize we were almost at my guesthouse. "What were you thinking? You looked very serious."

I shook my head, forcing myself to let go of all the worrying for now. "Oh, just making a mental list of all the things I need to get done before I leave. But I guess I'll just figure it all out while I'm in the office. It'll be hard to say goodbye to Tsehay and Bonnie," I said regretfully. "You'd think after years of doing this it would get easier. But there's something about doing this kind of work. People bond fast and strong."

He nodded in understanding and squeezed my knee gently. "First, we go on our hike to Entoto tomorrow. Then we can worry about the future."

The lump in my throat didn't let me respond with words, but I ran my hand over his thigh freely now that it was just the two of us in the truck—and I hoped that was answer enough.

We drove into the parking lot of the guesthouse in a comfortable silence, and within minutes I was standing in the lobby unsure of how to say goodbye after weeks of touching him until I had my fill.

He smiled at me, his hands in his pockets. "I have to spend the evening with my parents."

I looked up at him, trying hard return the smile, despite the ache of the moment. "I'll see you tomorrow morning, right?"

He beamed at the mention of the hike. I knew he was excited to show me another one of his favorite spots in the land he loved so much. "I'll be here at 8:00 a.m. Have a good night, konjo."

He leaned in, and for a moment my breath caught in the way it did whenever he was about to kiss me. The anticipation was not a bit less electric even after so many of them. But he caught himself in time and raised a hand to me instead. His eyes were remorseful, and I mirrored his gesture as he turned to go.

* * *

THE NEXT MORNING Elias drove us up to Entoto on a paved road that ended across from a large Ethiopian orthodox church about halfway up the mountain. The church was stunning. Built in the shape of a hexagon from wood cut in the nearby forest, it was huge, and looked like a box of chocolates hidden among the eucalyptus trees. It was painted in bright colors: the outside walls in an ocean blue, the awnings in bright yellows and reds. I observed the priests, a familiar sight by now, walking by wrapped in white linen robes and holding colorful umbrellas with golden fringe to protect themselves from the sun.

It was quite a sight to encounter on this misty, quiet mountain. I'd brought my camera with me, planning to capture some views of the city from up here, but I was going to fill my memory card before we got to the trailhead.

I smiled at Elias as I snapped some photos. "These churches are something."

He nodded. "You'll see many more when you're in the north," he said, mentioning my solo trip to see some of the historical sites. Just another reminder that our time was running out. As I looked up at him, I couldn't even imagine what it would be like to not see him again.

His eyes softened as if he could see into my thoughts. I could tell he was debating what to do, and in the end he squeezed my shoulder, his voice soft and warm when he finally spoke.

"There's a lot more to see, konjo."

Every time he called me that I still practically swooned. But I managed to hide it by snapping a few more pictures.

He ran a hand over my shoulder to get my attention, and his voice was a little amused when I looked up at him. "Let's start walking. We're not even four meters from the car, and you've taken a hundred photos."

I smiled at his teasing and started walking. "Hey, it's not my fault there are like, a million Insta moments happening right now."

He just shook his head and smiled. I *was* looking forward to this day. Even though I'd been in the country almost two months, mostly I'd been in the south. I hadn't seen much of Addis, and being here with Elias was perfect. He'd brought sandwiches, water, and packets of cookies so we could have a picnic after we got to the summit. I was feeling all of this a bit more than I should have, but I couldn't help myself. He paid attention to everything.

On the very first trip to Awassa, I'd mentioned in passing I had a weakness for chocolate-covered digestive biscuits. Since then he made sure to always have some on hand. When I commented on it, he just brushed it off and said, "I pay attention to what you like."

If and when it came to it, walking away from Elias was going to destroy me.

As we trekked up the mountain, we saw women carrying wood, which was a common sight all over Ethiopia. There was a large group of them and they each made their way down the mountain with massive piles of firewood on their backs, so big their torsos were almost perpendicular to the ground. I stopped to watch them as they hurried down the hill at an impressive clip, their eyes focused straight ahead.

"This group must have started late," Elias said. "Usually the wood is carried much earlier in the day. They need it for cooking, and to boil water for tea and baths." Elias stared after them too, then sighed. "Women's lives can be harsh here. At times it feels like they literally and figuratively carry us all on their backs. Not that there isn't progress—the economy is growing, and so many Ethiopians are coming back from overseas and starting businesses here—but there is still so much to do."

I nodded. "It can feel overwhelming. In the States too, so many things are totally broken. I've been thinking a lot about it in the last couple of months. Like, why am I here, and not there? Why do I get to come here or any other country and come up with solutions to problems I sometimes don't even understand? Meanwhile while my own country's systemic oppression is literally destroying lives and communities."

I blushed, embarrassed by my outburst. "I don't think I'm making sense."

He turned his head, considering my words. "I think you're right. In the end, you need to do the work you're passionate about. I don't agree with this idea that in order to do meaningful work, or to be successful, you have to be miserable, sacrifice everything. That to figure out ways to do good, I have to martyr myself. Purpose is noble, but it can't fill you up."

It felt wrong to have this conversation without touching. I wanted to put my head on his chest, breathe him in while he spoke the words I needed so badly to hear.

"You have to do the work that feeds you, find the joy in it."

I shuddered, feeling the truth of what he'd said in my bones. Before I could stop myself, I looked up at him and whispered, "I'm right here. You've found Joy."

He brushed my shoulder and looked at me with an intensity that shook me, then quietly said, "You are, and I did."

"You're like some kind of mystic. How do you have so much more wisdom than me and we're only a few years apart?"

He shook his head and bumped my shoulder again. "You're a lot wiser than you think."

* * *

WE SLOWLY MADE our way up the mountain until we reached the highest viewpoint and sat down to have our lunch. There were other families there and some young people, both Ethiopian and foreigners, were scattered around. We chatted with some of them and helped with photos when selfies would not do the view justice.

Once we sat down, Elias and I talked about how we were at the end of Ethiopian summer. Soon the rains would come, making everything muddy and wet for months.

When he had all our food out, we sat with our backs against a boulder, basking in the sun. From our spot we could see the sprawling city below. A hodge-podge of concrete, roads and mountains. Cars and buses weaving through mazes of tight cobblestone streets mixed with modern highways. It was quite the place. Addis Ababa. The New Flower. In my time here I'd grown to understand why my father loved this place as much as he did. And that connection to him was everything.

We ate our sandwiches and enjoyed the warm sun on our skin for a while. I was lying down on a blanket Elias had produced from his backpack and had my head pillowed on my folded jacket. I felt so content, I could've fallen asleep.

I was thinking that Elias still had not mentioned how it had gone with his parents the night before and was debating whether to ask when I saw him pull out a book from his backpack. He lay back propped on his elbow and started reading a poem out loud.

At first I didn't recognize it, then realized he was reciting Langston Hughes. Of course he was. I closed my eyes with a smile on my lips and listened as he read quietly, his lilting accent bringing the familiar words to life for me in a completely new way.

When ma man looks at me,
He knocks me off ma feet.
He's got those 'lectric-shockin' eyes an'
De way he shocks me sho is sweet.

I let him finish the poem before opening my eyes, locking them with his. I let him see how much I was feeling the poem. Him. This moment.

My man.

God, I wish he could be. He disarmed me with how open he was, how tenacious. To take the chance to kiss or touch me when he could never really know what my intentions were. He couldn't know for sure if I'd betray him. He just trusted I wouldn't. I turned to him as he leafed through the book, my head brimming with questions.

"That night at Saba's, why did you kiss me in front of her?" I asked, almost in a whisper, even though no one was close enough to overhear. I wanted to keep these words right in the space between us.

"Because you were waiting for my kiss, and I wanted to give it to you."

I turned my face away, but not so much that he couldn't see my smile. That was the truth, and he said it, and that's where Elias would end me: he would never lie to me.

I had to be brave enough to tell the truth too. I had to tell Elias how I felt about him. Even if it was only that: just something I had to say.

* * *

AFTER A WHILE WE gathered our stuff and walked back down to the car, and Elias drove me to the guesthouse. It was early afternoon and there weren't many people around, so I asked him if he'd stay for a bit. He didn't answer, just followed me up the stairs. Once inside, he locked the door, then turned around and raked his eyes over me with such heat I felt my skin burning.

We both took a step forward and met by the bed, grabbing at each other frantically. I lifted up on to my tiptoes so I could kiss him. We touched with urgency, like we were going to lose our minds if we didn't get as close as possible.

I licked into Elias's mouth one last time before going down on my knees in front of him. Having his cock in my mouth had become an obsession. I loved how into it Elias got. He went from gentle to rough and demanding as soon as I took him in my mouth. He'd grab the back of my head with both hands and push himself deep into my throat. Until all I could taste and smell was him.

I was hungry for that right now, to feel the intensity of this desire.

I looked up at him as I mouthed his crotch, the fabric of his shorts damp from pre-come.

"Give me your cock. I need it." I nosed at it, teasing. Not touching, wanting him to take out his dick and feed it to me.

He tugged on my hair just hard enough to make me pay attention. Lifting my face to look at him. His face was flushed, and his brown lips were tinted with pink where I'd bitten him. "If I have to pull it out and do all the work for you, I'm going to make you take it all at once."

The way he talked to me cranked me up to a fever pitch in no time. I was practically vibrating from how bad I needed him. "Do it."

He pushed his shorts down and took out his cock, the head pink and wet, foreskin pulled back. I almost listed, feeling the blood rushing to my ears. I stuck my tongue out, desperate to taste him, but before I did I raised my eyes to him. "I want you in my mouth, and then I want you to fuck me."

Elias's eyes widened, and his hand, which had been stroking my face, froze. "Are you sure?"

"Yes." Even though Elias and I had been together many times, we'd both set an unspoken boundary around that. What we'd already been doing was so good that I hadn't questioned why I didn't ask for more, and he'd let me set the pace. Maybe it was some silly line in the sand I created to protect myself from the inevitable. But he was already all the way inside my heart, and I wanted all of him.

He pulled on my hair again until I was looking straight at him. He bent down to give me a bruising kiss. Our tongues glided together until we were both gasping for air. When we pulled apart, his eyes were burning. "Open your mouth, Desta. I'm going to push in until I can feel your throat."

I moaned, desperate for it, and opened my mouth as he pressed inside. This was what I loved about Elias and me together. I was always vacillating, unsure if I could trust what I wanted, what my lover would think of me. Elias took me out of all of that. His touch brought together what I needed and what I wanted, and every caress was a confirmation that we were perfect together.

He let out a shuddering breath as he rammed his cock in my mouth, both hands firmly gripping the back of my neck. He gave me no quarter as he pushed inside. My eyes watered, but I kept taking him in. He thrust in a couple of times, his mouth in a flat line and his eyes rolling as he fucked my face.

"So pretty, those pink lips around me. God, you can suck cock."

I moaned again and he unclasped one of his hands to run a finger over the side of my face. "I'm going to fuck into your mouth, but when

I'm ready to come, I'm going to bend you over that bed and give you this cock until you scream my name."

That's what I wanted. That's what I *needed* right now. I hummed in approval, making him hiss and push in hard again.

Elias must have been feeling as desperate as I was. After a couple more thrusts, he pulled out and lifted me to him, kissing me as he walked us to the bed.

"We're wearing too many clothes," I gasped, and I started tugging the fleece over his head as he toed off his hiking shoes. After Elias was naked, I stood back to admire him as I made quick work of my clothes. Pretty soon we were standing in front of each other, completely bare. I'd seen his body so many times by now, touched every inch of it. Licked and nipped at leisure. This felt different.

This was *more*.

I reached out to him, his long, rangy body such a contrast to my stockier build, but we fit perfectly. He was everything I needed.

Without a word I got on the bed and lay on my stomach, ready for him. In the midst of the lust, there was a hint of something that felt so right, like this was exactly where I needed to be. That this man would always be what I needed. I didn't want to think about me leaving or his worries right now. This was just for us.

I heard his breath catch as I rested my head on my forearms, then felt his hands running down my spine. "Tell me you're mine, konjo."

"I *am* yours." I felt no hesitation, the words leaving my lips before my mind could catch up. He was wider than me, not bulky but strong, and when he rested his chest against my back I felt like we would combust, our skins were so hot pressed together. He brought his hand down to my ass and rubbed his finger against my hole, making me shiver.

"Are you going to let me in here?" He asked the question as his fingers brushed against the furled skin around my rim.

"Yes," I panted as he pressed a dry finger very gently against my opening.

"First, I'm going to love you with my tongue and fingers. Get you ready for me."

"I want that, so much."

He thrust against me and I could feel his cock brush my ass. "I can't wait to be so deep inside you. You won't be able to think about anything that isn't how full you are of me."

"Ungh." I pushed myself up and spread my legs wider. "Why do you hate me?"

Elias let out a startled laugh as he knelt behind me, his mouth so close to where I needed him, but still not touching. He ran his teeth over my ass cheek as he used his hands to spread me open.

"You're evil," I said, barely able to speak at this point.

His laugh only got filthier the more I whined. Soon he was lapping at my taint and the sensitive skin around my rim with his tongue, and I was burning for him to be inside. With Elias's hands on me, everything always felt so much easier, but there was an urgency right under the ease that never seemed to diminish.

"Please, baby, just *touch* me. With your fingers, with your tongue, your cock. I don't care."

I felt his tongue probing at my hole, then his finger spreading me open for his mouth, and I collapsed. My arms gave out on me as I made a sound I hardly recognized as my own voice.

"Mmm, konjo, you always taste so good. I like your balls too." He moved from my hole and popped one of my testicles into his mouth, fingers still probing at my ass. I was so overstimulated I felt like I was going to come apart. He hummed in appreciation after a particularly long stroke of this tongue. All I could do was push my ass at him to get more of what he was doing.

After another minute of his assault on my balls and ass, he moved away and I yelped at the loss of sensation. "Where are you going?"

Before he could answer, I heard the suction noise of the lube bottle as he pumped some out, and my heart started racing in anticipation. Within seconds I felt his silky-warm finger pressing against me, opening me up.

"That's so good, baby. I love your fingers." I squeezed my ass hard and he hissed.

"So tight, konjo. Is that what you're going to do when I'm inside

179

you?" As he talked he painted my ass with his dick, pre-come clinging to my skin.

In response I circled my hips exactly like I'd do it if I were riding him. "I'm going to milk your cock so good, you'll never want anyone else again."

This time he pushed his finger in to the second knuckle and bit down hard on my ass. "Who said I want anyone else now?"

I didn't answer. I was so caught up in the sensation of his hands on me, the heat of his body searing my skin. He worked two fingers in and out until he was pressing against my prostate, making me pant.

"Now. Now. Now." I sounded frantic, and I felt it too. Desperate for him.

A moment after I heard the tear of a condom wrapper and felt him work more lube in my hole. After a second I felt the blunt head of his cock pushing in and almost sobbed with relief.

"You're so tight." Elias sounded winded as he pressed in. I pushed back against the burn, meeting his thrusts until we were in perfect sync. Him pushing in, and me rocking back to meet him. Soon he was all the way in and we both sighed with relief. Elias pressed his chest to my back, our bodies so close.

"Desta," he gasped, breathless.

He bit down hard on my shoulder as he seated himself to the hilt. He had his hand at my nape and the other on the mattress, and fucked me so thoroughly I couldn't make words. After a few thrusts he grabbed my hips, lifting me up and pushing into me from an angle that hit me right where I needed it, making my entire body pulse.

"Oh, I'm gonna come like this. Fuck me harder, baby."

He bent down again and bit that same spot on my shoulder. "Make yourself come," he growled, his lips right by my ear.

"You're so fucking bossy." I laughed as I took my dick in hand. After just a few strokes, molten sensation spread through my groin, and soon I was coming, hot liquid splashing my hand.

Elias let out a pained gasp as he fucked me with short jabs. "So close."

I felt the heat of his come filling the condom a second before he slumped over me, his lips brushing the back of my neck.

We stayed like that for a while until our breaths evened out, then Elias shifted so he was on his back with my head on his chest.

"I don't think I can move for a while," I mumbled against his skin.

He chuckled as he ran his hand over my back. "I'm not in a rush to go anywhere," he whispered as he gathered me in his arms, tightening them. "We can stay here for now."

I placed my palm on his chest, fantasizing that this could be us forever. That we could make love and lay in a sunny room, unrushed and unbothered. That this wasn't a clandestine, temporary thing. I wished we could walk out of this room hand in hand without fear into the streets of this city Elias loved so deeply. One I was learning to love, too.

Maybe someday.

I felt Elias's lips brushing against my forehead, and then he asked in a quiet voice, "What's going on in there?"

I shook my head, not wanting to ruin the moment. "Just happy to be here with you."

He made a sound like he didn't quite believe me, but didn't respond right away. After a few breaths he spoke again. "I'd like you to come to my home and meet my parents tomorrow."

I sat up fast, hoping my face didn't look as spooked as I felt while Elias smiled placidly.

"Did I scare you?" He asked the question like he hadn't just said some earth-shattering shit to me.

I threw my hands up and scoffed. "Uh, well, I'm just a little shook. When you say meet your parents, does that mean in person?"

He rolled his eyes at the ridiculous question, still looking way too amused for the topic of conversation.

I paused before I asked the next question, not quite sure what kind of answer I was hoping. "Did you tell them?"

Again with the smiling. "I haven't told them yet, but I'm planning to after they meet you. I want them to know who the man I love is when I do."

181

I was glad I was already in bed because that would've certainly knocked me on my ass.

"For fuck's sake, Elias," I wailed before throwing my arms around his neck and kissing him hard. "Of course you'd say it first."

He threw his head back and laughed. "You're angry because I said I love you?"

I shook my head and kissed him again. "I wouldn't say angry, just frustrated that once again, I didn't get my shit together and you just did what I've been agonizing over for weeks now."

"Konjo." The word was a caress, a loving rebuke, and a prayer all in one, and I was so fucking gone for him. I pressed our foreheads together before I spoke again, wanting to be as close as possible to him as I could.

I didn't know if we'd be able to be together after I left here in a few weeks. If Elias would really come out to his family and leave Ethiopia. If I'd be strong enough to tell my mother the truth about what I wanted to do. I didn't know anything for sure other than what I felt for him right now.

I could say *that* with certainty, and I did.

"I love you too."

CHAPTER 24

As we pulled up to the big metal fence of Elias's family home, I wondered if he felt as nervous as I did. But when I looked at him with his back straight, his head up, he seemed so resolute and certain, *so certain*. Meanwhile, I was doing my best to keep my shit together.

After our big confession the day before, Elias had stayed with me until dinnertime and then gone home with the promise to pick me up for dinner tonight. He had a lot take care of and I needed to buy some supplies for my trip north in a couple of days. My time in Ethiopia was wrapping up and the dread of going back to reality was starting to get the best of me. But tonight wasn't about my shit, it was about Elias. I was determined to be here for him in every way.

We drove into the compound where his family lived, and before we were even out of the car, a beautiful woman who I assumed was his mother walked out of the house to greet us. She was wearing a traditional Amhara dress in white cotton with beautiful gold, red, and green embroidery running from the center of the neckline down to the hem. She also had traditional jewelry on. Gold earrings that looked like a sun and a small cross hanging from a necklace on her chest that I knew was the one from the Amhara tribe. All indications that she considered me an important guest, which only made my already-galloping heart speed up.

"Hello, Desta. Welcome to our home. I'm Negash. Eli has told us so much about you."

I went in for a triple kiss and embrace. The more kisses, the more respect you were showing an elder, and I wanted to express my deepest regard to his parents.

"It's so nice to meet you. Thank you for inviting me to dinner." I handed over the bottle of Chivas Regal and box of chocolates Saba had recommended I bring with me.

Negash held up the box and smiled. "This is very nice of you, Desta." After saying my name, her expression changed, and suddenly she was beaming at me. "I could not believe when Eli told me his American friend had a Habesha name."

She chuckled at my shy nod as we walked into the house. The living room was well lit, with a huge black leather sectional couch, where an older man in jeans and a starched button-down shirt was sitting and watching a soccer match. He looked like Elias, but seemed a lot older than his mom.

When he saw me, he stood up to shake my hand. "Welcome to our home. I am Fikru Bekele."

I gripped his forearm and bumped his shoulders in greeting. "Thank you. I'm grateful for your invitation, Mr. Bekele."

He waved off my formality, extending his hand to the couch, offering me a seat. "Just Fikru, please."

In that moment, it struck me that in Ethiopia, a person's surname was their father's first name. The Western way was similar, but it seemed like a much more profound connection to share the name your father answers to on a daily basis.

Fikru glanced over at Elias, who was looking at us from the door. "My son never brings any friends home. We were surprised when he told us we'd have a visitor." His father's face turned rueful as he sat back down. "I embarrass my son sometimes when I talk too much."

Elias pushed up from the door and gave his father a concerned look. "Aba."

The man waved him off with a friendly gesture and went back to what was happening on the screen. I'd been to a few Ethiopian homes already and knew that the TV being on while there were visitors was pretty common, so I took a seat on the couch, and soon Elias brought out a tray with drinks. His mom came out after a moment too, and we all started to get to know each other.

"Desta, tell me about you parents. Eli said you lived here as a baby."

I nodded. "Yes, we left around the time I turned three. My parents lived here the first year they got married, then returned right after I was born a couple of years later."

Negash grinned, obviously delighted at my family's connection to her country. "They must have liked it here."

I nodded as I put down the glass of cold Ambo and Coke that Elias had handed me. I tried to ignore the flutter happening in my chest caused by Elias's gesture of getting me my preferred drink, and focused my attention on his mother. "Yes, my dad especially. He always called Ethiopia the homeland of his heart."

"Sounds like he was a man with a good soul," she said regretfully. Elias must have told them about his death.

"He was."

After that the conversation turned to the meal and the soccer match. A moment later the cook—having house help was also a common thing in Ethiopia—started bringing out dishes and we moved to the table. Soon we were all digging into the meal, which was delicious. "This is really good. Thank you again." I said as I pinched of a mouthful of injera and sautéed Swiss chard off my plate.

Negash beamed at me and put more food on my plate. I thanked her and turned to Elias, who looked tense, and had been quieter than usual. "Where's your sister tonight?"

Before he had a chance to answer, his dad spoke up in a dejected tone. "My children are always finding reasons to escape this house."

Elias gave his dad a worried look but didn't react to his comment. "They've been looking for a house. Tonight they're meeting with one of her husband's cousins, who's building some homes right down the street. They'll still be very close." That last part seemed a lot more for his dad's benefit than mine.

Elias's dad seemed genuinely upset by this. "Why does she need to leave?" Everyone tensed as he got more agitated, but no one said anything, and he kept talking. "When are you leaving, Eli? Are you escaping soon too?"

His tone wasn't even angry, but it seemed like it was the needle that broke the camel's back for Elias. His mom said something in Amharic, which I assumed was aimed at his dad. Whatever it was it seemed to mollify the man, but after a moment Elias stood up and excused himself. The tension in the room was so heavy I could almost see it. I soon did the same with a barely audible "excuse me" and followed Elias outside.

I found him standing in a dark corner of the yard with his hands in his pockets, looking up at the starry sky. "Hey."

He turned when he heard me, but didn't say anything. I stood next to him in silence, and after a moment he spoke. "I knew this would happen. I haven't told him yet, but I think he suspects I'm leaving. I've been running errands and getting my things in order. My mother too. She wants me to go, though."

His eyes were so bleak. All I wanted was to hold him. "My father thinks if we go, we do it because he embarrasses us." He shook his head in obvious frustration. "It's not true. I love my father. I just need to *go*."

The pain in his voice broke my heart into a million pieces. I wished there was something I could say, but I knew there wasn't anything that could make this decision less agonizing for Elias. I touched his shoulder, and I could feel the tension ease a little. "I'm so sorry, baby."

"There's nothing you need to apologize for, and thank you for coming tonight. I needed you to meet them." He sighed and looked up again. "I don't know how any of this will go, but I have to speak my truth. I can't—"

He choked on that word, and I moved closer. We were hidden by a hedge of trees where we were standing. I moved so I was facing him and put my arms around his waist, my head against his chest.

"I'm so tired of hiding." His voice was strangled, and I could feel the misery rolling off him in waves as he tightened his arms around me. "But every time I get close to telling them, I feel like it will be irreversible."

"I know," I said lamely, not sure if anything could make this better.

We stood here for a few seconds, and when I tried to pull back he kept me there, a strong arm around me. "Stay."

"Elias, I don't know if we should—"

"Please," he pleaded as he lifted my chin with his hand.

He kissed me. And as always, from the first taste I was lost.

I heard the surprised gasp first, but what made me jump back from Elias was the loud crash that followed it. We looked up and found Elias's mother who was looking at us from a few feet away in complete horror. Her hands were suspended in the air, and there were shards of glass scattered in front of her on the ground. It looked like she'd been bringing us something to drink when she saw us.

"Mama."

She shook her head, and her voice came out thin and strangled. "Elias, this is not how you do things. No, my son. This is not how you do things." She stumbled forward and the crunch of the glass under her feet sounded like thunder, so loud in our horrified silence. After a moment she looked down at her feet, she seemed dazed, like she had no idea how the wreckage of glass and ice got there. After giving us a final glance, she walked back to the house.

I looked after Negash, feeling like my heart was going to crawl up my throat. I turned to Elias, who hadn't moved or said a word since his mom came out. The way his mouth contorted, but could not make words, as if the realization of what he'd just done had robbed him of the ability to speak, made me finally start moving.

"You need to go talk to her. I'll go home," I said numbly.

I started walking fast toward the gate of the compound without daring to look in the direction of the house, overcome with guilt and dread that I'd brought this down on Elias. "I'm taking off, okay? I'll go out to the main road and get a taxi. I'll call you later."

I heard the crunch of the glass, and suddenly I felt Elias's hand gripping my elbow.

"Desta. Stop." He sounded so desperate and so lost that I froze. The need in his voice kept me from running. I had to dig my fingernails into my hands in order to keep from reaching out for him.

Touching him like that out here in the open was not an option, so I moved away. He let go of my elbow, and then we started moving toward the car. "I will take you home."

We both got in, and I had to push the heel of my hand into my chest. My heart was beating fast and my breaths were coming in short pants. I was convinced I'd ruined everything for Elias. His relationship with his parents, his departure to the States. His life. His future. I'd fucked up everything.

I opened my mouth and what came out was a croak. When I tried again, my voice sounded small and scared. "I'm so sorry."

Elias was still silent, and he gripped the steering wheel of the car with such force I thought he was going to snap it off with his bare hands. I could see him trying hard to control his breathing, his eyes closed tightly. After a few more seconds I saw his shoulders loosen, and he opened his eyes to look at me. They were like embers, hot with whatever he was feeling.

"*Never be sorry*. Never be sorry for touching me or loving me." His voice gave out then, and despite my fear that his would make everything worse, I kissed him, because I couldn't not reach for him if he needed me.

Our mouths met in a chaste kiss and we pressed our foreheads together. "What's going to happen now? I'm scared I've made everything worse by coming here."

He shook his head forcefully. His hands interlocked at the back of my neck. "No. Don't say that. I need to talk to them and I don't know what will happen, but I can't lie anymore."

He let go and sat straight again. When I looked toward the house, his mother and father were standing by the window. "There are some things I need help with so I can go to New York. I was going to ask my parents and my sister. Now I don't know if that will happen. I don't know if I'll be able to walk away from my parents and leave things like this."

That was like a punch in the gut, because once again Elias was telling me the truth, never promising things that would make him betray what he'd said to me. "I don't know much about anything, but I am certain that I'll never be sorry for you."

I nodded, literally biting my tongue from the need to beg him to assure me that we would be all right, that this would not be the last time I saw him. I needed to not add to the already overwhelming weight on his shoulders, to not be one more person in his life burdening him with their own needs and wants. I sat there, barely able to take a breath, knowing the hope I'd been harboring in the past few weeks had to be snuffed out, for both our sakes.

I felt someone shaking me, and I looked up. "Desta. I'm going to go inside to tell my mother I'm taking you home."

"Okay." I watched Elias get out of his car and walk up to his house, his shoulders straight and his head high, face determined. Looking at him being so brave, I swore to myself that if I ever got the chance to be with this man, I would do everything in my power to live up to that kind of courage and dignity.

* * *

HE WAS ONLY in the house a few minutes before he got back in the car and drove us out of the compound. His face was completely expressionless. I was too scared to ask how it went, so I sat in silence until we arrived at my guesthouse.

I assumed Elias would leave me by the entrance and head home, but he parked the car inside and got out with me. All the way up the stairs, the heavy silence was suffocating. I opened the door to the room and Elias walked inside as I followed him in.

As soon as the door was locked, we moved toward each other and embraced, Elias gripping me with such force that I almost whimpered.

I was afraid to ask if this was goodbye. I was so scared I would never see him again.

"Konjo, I'm going to go soon, and I can't promise you that I will see you before you return home. I have things to take care of so I can go to New York."

I nodded as I held on to him my eyes shut tightly. "Okay. I know."

He shook his head. "Desta, look at me."

I didn't want to. I wanted to hide, knowing in my heart this was the end. That once again I had done this to myself. Put my heart out to be destroyed and in the process, brought along someone else who could face terrible consequences.

A sob escaped my throat, and Elias pulled back. "Don't cry, konjo, please. Don't cry for me."

"I'm afraid I'll never see you again," I said, feeling so fucking miserable.

"Shhh." He made soothing noises, looking at me with concern, but still he didn't tell me I was wrong in thinking we were over. I squeezed my eyes shut, forcing my tears to dry, to stop this.

When I looked at him his face was serious, but he wasn't shying away from what he needed to say. "I can't make you a promise I do not know I can keep, but it's not because I don't love you."

I couldn't speak, but Elias went on. "It may not be soon, but we *will* see each other again."

I glanced up at him and barely saw him with my eyes full of tears. "What if it's not the same?" I asked, unable to hold all my doubts from spilling out.

"It won't be the same. Our time together like this is over. We may have a chance at something different." He lifted a shoulder, clearly as unsure as I was about any future for us. "But you must believe in what we made together."

How was he this strong?

I shuddered out a breath. "Okay."

We embraced again, and our kisses tasted so much like sorrow. Like an ending.

I watched out the window of my room as Elias got in his car and drove away, going home to face his parents and tell his truth. I wiped my eyes with my sleeve and grabbed my laptop, which was sitting on my desk, and decided to Skype my mother.

Like Elias, before I could start the next part of my life, I needed to come clean to the person who mattered the most to me. Even if it meant breaking her heart.

CHAPTER 25

As I readied to call my mom, my mind raced, thinking about Elias and the agony he was clearly going through. Yet he was determined to tell his parents everything before he left Ethiopia. No matter how things turned out, he was willing to face the consequences in order to live his truth. And here I was just days from having to go back to the States, still as lost as I'd been when I got here.

That wasn't true though. *I knew.* I'd known before I got on the plane in DC. And what was more, I was ready. I just needed to show up to my own life and stop using the people I loved as excuses to not live for myself.

Determined, I opened the Skype app and clicked the icon to video call my mother. After only a few seconds, I saw her smiling face.

"Mijo."

I smiled back at her and took a deep breath. "Hey, Mamí. I wanted to tell you about how my plans have changed."

She widened her eyes and brought her face closer, worry lines etched around her mouth. "Are you all right? You're worrying me, Desta."

I shook my head, resisting the urge to reassure her, to say whatever I needed to in order to make her relax. I thought about Elias driving back to his family and how scary it had to be to do it alone. But it was how it had to be, no one could do this for him. He had to do it for himself, and I had to do the same.

"I don't think I'm going to take the new job." My vision blurred from holding my breath and my heart pounded in my chest. This was what I'd promised myself I'd never do: never give my mother a reason to be sad, to feel like another part of my father was dying.

"Oh?" She cocked her head, as if she was trying to read what was going on inside my head. "Did something happen? Are you staying in Addis longer?"

I shook my head and brought my knees up to my chest. "No, I just —I think I want to go to grad school, do something different." I closed my eyes and just said it. "I think I want to do social work school. There's a program at NYU that focuses on working with refugee children in the States. I think that's what I want to do. I like this work a lot…"

I looked at the screen and my mom's face was serious, but the faraway look she had told me she was thinking hard. Trying to figure out what I wasn't ready to say yet. Finally, she turned her eyes to the screen. "Desta Joy, I think you need to hear me say this." She paused then, clearing her throat, obviously bracing herself. "There is nothing more important to me than for you to be happy." She clicked her tongue in that way she did when she thought things were in a sorry state. "We've lost too much, mi amor, to waste time on things that don't fulfill us."

A knot closed my throat when I heard the same words Elias had said to me coming from my mother.

I wanted to believe her, and at the same time I didn't. I wasn't sure I'd know what to do if the burden of living out this dream for my mother disappeared. Before I knew it, I was blurting it all out. "I fell for this guy here."

"Oh, Desta." My mother's voice was completely devoid of any judgment, and that was almost worse.

I shook my head, hardly able to process everything that had happened tonight, but it was still bursting out of me. I wanted so much, and I needed my mother to be there for me. "He's on the team for the project, but he got into a PhD program at Columbia and I don't know if I'm doing all of this for me, or just as an excuse to go to New York and follow him."

My mother opened her mouth, closed it. Then she sat up straighter. "Does it matter?"

I snapped my head back at her question. That was not I was expecting. "What do you mean?"

"If you finally decided to do what you want, is it so bad that what pushed you was someone you care about?" She sounded genuinely confused.

"But I do this, Mom. I keep getting into relationships that can't work out. Where I get my heart broken. Elias isn't even sure he can come to the States, he's got family to think about, and now I've complicated my own plans by getting involved with him."

My mother shook her head and I could see that doing this over video was starting to frustrate her. "Desta Joy, you can be falling in love and still want to make these changes. Both can happen at the same time, baby."

Maybe. It *was* true that I'd applied for that MSW program long before Elias was in the picture.

"I just don't want to be some pathetic fool."

"You're not pathetic."

I deflated at the fierce urgency in my mother's voice and heard the echo of Elias's plea for me to believe in what we had made. I couldn't discard that.

"You say that, but I keep chasing after men who drop me when I'm no longer a convenient part of their plan." But even as I said it, I knew that wasn't remotely fair. Elias was not Miguel, and he would never do that. Even tonight, when everything was awful, he didn't try to reassure me by making promises he didn't know he could keep. He'd told me how he felt, promised me he'd fight, and then gone out to do it.

"You're right, I'm not pathetic, and I'll be fine. We both will." I felt stronger as I said it. The misery of the evening was already turning into purpose. I didn't know what, if anything, would happen to change how things ended with Elias tonight. But I would do what I needed for me. I'd make myself whole. I was on my way there already.

"We're both stronger than we give ourselves credit for." My mom's voice sounded a little surer too.

"We *are* strong." I wasn't sure if I was talking about my mother and me or Elias and me, but in that moment it didn't matter.

Tears were running down my mother's face, and for once I didn't feel compelled to stop them. "Tell me about your plans and your novio, sweetheart. I want to know."

I straightened, a sad little smile on my face at my mother's request to hear about my boyfriend, but then I started to tell her.

* * *

ONCE I FINISHED with my mom, I decided to hit up the other woman in my life and give her some news that was going to blow her away. Hopefully making plans would do something to soothe my battered heart.

DestaJoyWalker: Yo! Are you free for like a minute? I need you to tell me what the farthest point in NYC from where you live is so I can start looking for apartments there.

Within a second I could see she was typing.

Lucía.Woods: MIRA COÑO. WHY ARE YOU PLAYING WITH ME DESTA JOY? FUCK THIS MESSAGING SHIT!!!

I picked up the call after the first ring.

"What are you talking about?" She was yelling into the phone and I could hear noises like she was walking outside.

"I'm moving to New York."

"Please *do not* mess with me. Do you know what it would mean for me to finally be in the same city with you after all these years of weekly calls and text messages?"

I grinned into the phone, and despite how fucked-up the last two hours had been, I felt...relieved. "I'm going to do the MSW, Luce. I'm coming home, amiga."

I heard her breath catch over the phone and mine caught too, because with every conversation tonight I realized this move was exactly what I needed. Like my mother said, Elias had been what finally made me brave enough to go for it. And it was not lost on me that I had done the same for him.

"Oh my god, babe. You don't how happy I am right now. You got me crying on the fucking High Line, bro."

I chuckled at how annoyed she sounded. "Well, it's not all rainbows and sunshine right now. Luce, Elias's mother caught us kissing. He was going to tell them, but that was not how they should've found out." I cringed, remembering Negash's face when she saw us. "I have no idea if he's going to be okay or what's even happening. We had plans. I mean very tentative plans, but now I don't know."

She sighed on the speaker. "Shit. I'm sorry, hon. Do you think his family will be awful?"

"I don't know," I said, unsure. I knew one could never tell for sure how people would react to these things, but Elias's family loved him. No matter how complicated things seemed, it was clear they adored him. "I hope not. He *was* going to talk to them tonight anyway; he just wanted me to meet them first. He's accepted his spot at Columbia and so part of the plan was to come out to them as well. He didn't want to leave with that secret."

I heard Lucía's wheel turning from seven thousand miles away. "He's coming to New York? Desta, is that—"

"No, Lucía, I swear. This is about me. About what I want. I just told Mami before I called you. I need to do what makes me happy, Luce. I *need* to. Besides, Elias may not even be in New York this fall, not after how shitty things went tonight."

"Okay, babe," she said, clearly trying to appease me. "Of course, and you know you're going to stay with us until you find a place." I nodded like she could see me, but she didn't wait for an answer, already full steam ahead with planning. Just like I knew she would be. "Actually, you know what? Let me talk to Norma from work—she mentioned her brother needed to sublet his place for the summer. He's going to Spain for six months, and he's up by me. I'll email you."

"Okay, sounds good," I said, slightly less freaked out than I had been a few minutes before.

"So you'll be here in a few weeks?" she asked, the excitement in her voice making my own resurface.

"In nine days. I have my trip tomorrow and come back the day before I leave. I have to go to DC and sort out some stuff, but I fly into JFK anyways, so I'll stay for a few days to arrange the move."

"Are you going to be able to see your guy before then?" She sounded worried and sad for me.

I shook my head as if she could see me. "I don't know."

"Take care of yourself on that trip." She grumbled, "I don't want you getting eaten by a lion or some shit when I'm so close to having you back."

I cracked up. "There aren't lions where I'm going. Maybe a baboon."

"Whatever! Seriously, though, enjoy your trip and get back safe. Everything's going to work out. I know it will."

I really hoped she was right. "I'll talk to you soon."

I ended the call, and as I got ready for bed and packed the rest of the things I'd take north, I wondered how it was going with Elias and his family. I checked my phone and saw there were no messages, and couldn't decide if that was a good or bad thing.

I went to bed with a clear mind and very sore heart. But for the first time in a long time, I finally felt like I was looking forward to what was next.

CHAPTER 26

"Do you have everything, dear?"

I turned around from zipping my bag and nodded at Saba. I'd come to stay at her house when I returned from my trip the day before, and was now getting ready to head to the airport.

I pointed toward the hallway leading to the bedroom. "Just have to get my laptop bag. I'll be right back."

She waved me off. "Tefare is on his way. It's only 8:30 and your flight isn't until midnight. You have more than enough time."

Saba stood by the door of her guest bedroom and watched as I hurried to get the last of my things. "How are you feeling about leaving?"

Her tone told me she already knew.

I answered with my eyes focused on what I was doing, not feeling up to facing her knowing gaze. "Completely unprepared. The good-byes at the office were hard." In the morning I'd gone to say goodbye to Bonnie and the rest of the team at Aid USA. Even Sam had acted like a human when I stopped by his cubicle.

I heard Saba exhale from behind me. "You'll see them again." I expected that to sting, but it didn't. It felt inevitable that I would come back.

"You're right. I think I will." Everyone at Aid had given me multiple hugs and had made me promise I'd be back for a visit soon, and when I said I would, it felt like the truth.

While I was there, Bonnie had given me a couple of funny looks and told me to update her about my summer plans. I suspected she knew about Elias and me. The urge to ask her if she knew more than the little bits of information I'd gotten from him while I was travelling had been strong, but I would never betray his trust.

I grabbed my stuff and checked my phone one final time before I took out the SIM card.

No messages.

I'd exchanged a few texts and calls with Elias asking how things were going in the last few days. He'd said they were all right, but hadn't gone into too much detail. Today he'd finally said he unfortunately would not be able to see me.

I was disappointed—okay, more like gutted—but I'd done my best to be understanding. He needed to get his things in order. The plan was still for him to go to the States for school this fall, and I hoped it meant there was a chance for us as well. But I'd decided I needed to focus on myself, just as he was doing.

I'd told him I would be in New York after I talked to my mom, needing him to know I was ready for more. But even if it didn't work out, what I got to have with Elias was amazing. Still, it *would* crush me to not see him ever again, and I wasn't ready to think about that yet.

I headed to the door of the bedroom with my laptop in hand and gave Saba the SIM card with a sigh.

She clicked her tongue at my gloomy mood. "You must trust it will be okay."

She'd spent the day giving me pep talk after pep talk. I was getting a little exasperated, but smiled when she hissed at my stank face. I was about to reassure her once again that I was fine when we heard a car at the gate. Shortly after, the headlights of Tefare's old Lada were illuminating the dark yard.

I hefted it on my backpack and grabbed the tube, which held the rolled-up canvas I'd bought in the gallery at the Marquis. It cost me an arm and a leg, but it was the only thing I was taking back with me, other than a few pounds of coffee. I wasn't counting the broken heart and career change plans that would also be coming home with me.

I went over to where Saba was standing, looking a little weepy.

"Saba," I said, trying to convey a clear *don't do this*. She sniffled, pulling me in for a tighter hug, and I let out a flustered laugh, almost ready to cry myself. "No no no, none of that. You're coming to visit in December! Stop it!"

"Yes, I will see you and your mama for the holidays, but it's been so nice to have you here." She kissed my forehead and pulled back to look at me. "You've grown up so fine, Desta Joy. I'm so glad you finally came to see your other homeland. We want you back soon."

I nodded, swallowing down tears, certain I would return. "I'll be back."

Saba walked out to the car with me. I put my bag in the trunk and greeted Tefare with a few shoulder bumps.

"Are you ready to go home?" He smiled at me like he knew it was not an easy question to answer.

"I think so."

He shrugged, looking between me and Saba. "We will be waiting for you. You have this land in your heart and in your name."

"I do," I said, feeling the truth in his words.

I was about to get in the car when Saba touched my shoulder and pulled something out of her pocket. It was an envelope. On the back I saw the familiar handwriting, and just one word.

Konjo.

I took it from her slowly. "He was here?"

"He dropped it off the night before you got back." She gave me that same grin she'd been sending my way whenever Elias came up and raised her shoulder feigning innocence. "We've been getting to know each other."

I just stood there, dumbstruck while she wagged a finger at me. "Don't open it until you're on the plane."

I scoffed, glaring at her. "Are you kidding me?"

"He asked me to make you promise."

"Saba!" I could not believe this shit.

She waved me off smiling. "Get in the car. You'll miss your plane. I promise you don't want to read it now."

I blinked at her, still processing the last minute.

I opened my mouth to ask what her tone meant. She sounded amused, but there was certainly nothing to laugh about as far as I could tell. "So you're not going to tell me."

"I am not. And really, Desta, you need to get in the car," she said with urgency, ushering me toward Tefare.

"I thought you said I was fine with time," I huffed as I got in, but at the last second I blew her a kiss as we drove away, the envelope from Elias burning a hole in my jacket pocket.

After a few minutes we were on the road to the airport, and Tefare looked in the rearview mirror with a knowing expression on his face. "So? Did you find what you came looking for, Desta?"

I smiled and closed my eyes before I answered. "That and more, my friend."

* * *

I GOT to my gate with some time before boarding and found an empty chair to wait. Since I'd arrived at the airport, I'd been playing a game with myself to see how long I could go without tearing into Elias's note. I'd run a hand over it. Take it out of my pocket to make sure it was there. I moved it to my backpack and finally put it back where it was closest to me.

But now that the moment when I could read it was getting nearer, I felt afraid. What if this was just a final goodbye? What if he just didn't want to have to tell me in person? But I decided that it couldn't be that. Elias wouldn't do that to me.

I took a deep breath, reaching into my pocket, and pulled it out. I read the letters on the back again, ran my fingers over them.

I decided that no one needed to know if I opened it twenty goddamn minutes earlier than I was supposed to. How much fucking restraint was a person expected to have?

I pushed my finger under the flap, tore it open, then pulled out the paper. There were only three lines. I read them quickly, gasping as the words sank in.

I chose myself, konjo, and you, if you still want me.

I will see you very soon.

Love, Elias

I wasn't sure what that meant, but with everything in me I believed he would keep that promise.

I closed my eyes as tears streamed down my face, the tightness in my chest I'd been trying to ignore for days finally loosening. Sensing the meaning of those words seeping into my bones. The relief of being certain that I hadn't been in this alone.

In the distance I heard an announcement that they would start boarding in a few minutes, and I pocketed the note, trying to get myself together. Suddenly I felt someone standing close to me, and what sounded like Elias's low, husky chuckle coming from above.

"I told Saba you wouldn't wait."

I snapped my head up and saw him only a couple of feet away. He was wearing his leather jacket, gray scarf, red Chucks, and the most beautiful smile I had ever seen on his face. I stood up fast, knocking over my laptop bag, and almost jumped him before I remembered where I was.

I couldn't just kiss him. I had to keep my head. This was not me realizing my lover—who I thought I might never see again—was actually getting on the flight home with me. Elias and I couldn't be that to each other here. No, right now I was just saying hello to a friend.

Touching him always made everything simpler, so I closed the small distance between us as my body shook so violently my teeth chattered. I could see a flutter in Elias's cheek; he was working as hard as I was to keep from grabbing me.

"You're here," I gasped, still astonished he was standing in front of me.

That smile again. "I am, and I'm going to New York. I'll need to come back to Addis before classes start, but this is it…"

"Can we say a proper hello?" I asked, shaking like a leaf.

He let go of the death grip he had on the handle of his carry-on, and we moved to bump our shoulders together. As our bodies touched, I could feel the shivers running through him, and I was sure he could feel mine. We pressed together one shoulder, then the other, and finally thumped each other hard on the back.

"It's good to see you, Desta," he breathed out, and I could hear the depth of emotion he was feeling in the trembling in his voice.

I shuddered out a breath that felt like it was coming from the deepest place in my soul. "You too."

After a moment we separated and moved to sit beside each other, waiting for the plane to board. We had to look ridiculous with the giddy grins we both had on our faces, and I did not care in the slightest.

"So how did it go with your parents? I was so worried."

He shook his head, smiling sadly. "Better than I expected, actually. My dad especially has always prided himself on being counter-culture," he said, amused. "So he was pretty good about it. My mother was shocked, but she's coming around. Mostly they want me to be happy. I think it's also easier for them that I'll be in the States where things are better, at least when it comes to this. My sister already knew. Or at least she says she did."

I exhaled, the last bit of tightness melting off my shoulders. "I'm so glad."

He gave me a regretful look, and I saw him fist his hand from where it was right by mine. "I'm sorry I didn't get in touch, but once I decided I wanted to try to leave with you, I had a million things to do, and it wasn't certain until almost the last minute that I'd be able to pull it off. Saba was a lot of help. She was able to get my visa expedited, and Bonnie was great at helping me get all my paperwork in for my resignation from Aid. It's been hectic."

I shook my head in disbelief. "I can't believe no one told me anything! Traitors."

He laughed. "It was supposed to be a surprise."

"Well, I was shocked, so good job." I tried to sound annoyed, but I was so clearly ecstatic he wasn't buying it.

We sat there in silence, grinning at each other for the next couple of minutes, and with every second I got more desperate to get on the damn plane. Thankfully boarding started, and soon we were walking onto the plane together.

As we shuffled along the bridge, I felt like I was literally heading into a new life.

Once in the plane, we didn't have seats together, of course. I'd gotten an upgrade to business class and Elias was in the back of the plane. He looked at me ruefully and pointed in the direction of his seat. "I'll see you in New York City."

I balked and grabbed his jacket, refusing to let him out of my sight. "Hell no. We're sitting together. Here—" I said, looking at the seat number on his boarding pass. "Let's go to yours. I'll give mine to the person sitting next to you."

Now it was his turn to balk. "That's a business class seat. Why would you do that?"

I looked up at him with the most pissed-off face I could manage while also experiencing delirious levels of happiness. "Because the man I love is in row twenty-eight, and that's where I will be on this long-as-hell flight."

"Okay, Desta." He cracked up and kept shuffling along to the end of the plane. God, I wanted to weep. I thought I'd never hear him say my name again.

We got to his seat, which was in the middle of the plane. After a ten-second exchange, a very happy middle-aged Ethiopian man walked off to take my business class seat, and Elias and I took our aisle and window seats.

We got busy with the business of settling into a long flight, stowing luggage, getting the things we'd need, and chatting with other passengers. Soon they were announcing that the plane was closed and we were next for takeoff.

I placed the complimentary blanket over our laps and looked for Elias's hand under it. He clutched it tight and brought our intertwined hands out from under the covers, placing them right where everyone could see. I looked around worriedly, but he shook his head.

"No more hiding."

I nodded, my throat tightening. The plane taxied out before I could find my voice, and within seconds we were airborne.

Elias never let go of my hand.

I sat there waiting for the lights to go out, as if that were the sign, the confirmation this was actually happening.

As soon as they did, I turned around and pressed my face to his cheek. "I'm going to kiss you now."

He turned so that our lips were pressed to each other, and he mouthed the words.

Eshi, konjo.

EPILOGUE

New York City
August

"You're going to be late for your first day of class," I yelled from the kitchen.

After a few seconds Elias stepped out from our bedroom, looking delicious in a red T-shirt and jeans, his feet still bare. I smiled when I looked down at the "coffee bean" on his toe.

"If we're late, it's because someone woke up wanting to do things to me," he said playfully, and put his arms around my waist.

I shivered, remembering how many things I'd done to him this morning, right before he returned the favor.

Sometimes it still felt like a dream that we were here. That five months ago we'd left Ethiopia together and now were living in New York City.

As soon as we'd landed, it was as though our lives had never been separate. We'd gotten into the sublet Lucía found us, which we eventually took over because Norma's brother had decided to stay in Madrid for another year. We loved our little studio, and our neighborhood. Elias had gotten on great with Lucía and Moe, and loved working with his advisor. As for me, I had my first MSW class in the afternoon downtown at NYU, but before that I was going to my job as a counselor for an agency working with homeless LGBTQ youth. I loved everything about my job and could not wait to start my classes.

Elias squeezed me tight as he nosed my hair. "What are you thinking, konjo?"

"That I'm really fucking happy right now. Like 'pinch me, play the lotto' levels of happy."

He gave me that amused expression he sometimes had when I said something very farenji-sounding, and kissed me as he moved to get some coffee.

He passed me a mug and we stood there sipping our coffee and grinning at each other before we heard the ring from a Whatsapp call coming from Elias's phone. He grabbed it and smiled as he tapped on the screen.

"Is it your mom?"

He nodded and waved me over to where he was standing. I pressed in close to him and looked at her smiling face on the screen. "I wanted to wish you good luck in your first day. Both of you. We're so proud of you, Eli."

"Amaseganallo, Mama." His voice was full of emotion as he thanked her.

I nodded at her and did the same. "Thank you. We're excited to start."

She nodded at us with watery eyes as Elias's dad waved from his spot on the couch. Elias had returned home on his own over the summer, and that visit seemed to have made things easier with his parents. Over the past few months, communication with them had gotten more and more comfortable, and these days, most of the calls involved easy smiles and lots of teasing about Elias's new American life.

"Call me tomorrow to tell me how it went, Eli. You, too, Desta."

We both agreed and said our goodbyes. Soon we were grabbing our bags and heading out the door. We walked out to a sunny summer day in Manhattan. It was only seven thirty in the morning, but humidity was probably at a hundred percent already. I was sweating by the time we took our first step onto the pavement, hand in hand. We walked the two blocks to the train together as we always did, and once again I could barely believe this was my life.

We got to the corner and moved to the side so we could say goodbye. I would take the train a few stops uptown to 161st Street, and he'd go across the street to catch the downtown one to 116th. Like he did every day, Elias grabbed my face and kissed me goodbye.

"Have a good day. See you at home, konjo."

As I stood at the entrance to the subway, I turned around to look at him one more time, and called out as he crossed the street, "Eshi, love."

* * *

THANK YOU FOR READING, DON'T MISS MY NEXT RELEASE!

Sign up to my newsletter for updates.

Reader reviews are incredibly helpful in helping others find new books to enjoy and only take a moment to leave. Please leave a review.

FOR MORE INFO ABOUT THE AUTHOR VISIT
ADRIANAHERRERAROMANCE.COM

AUTHOR'S NOTE

My partner and I moved to Addis Ababa, Ethiopia only a couple of months after we got married. We were there for a year and then returned when our daughter was just a few months old, and lived there until she was three. Just like Desta's father I consider Ethiopia the homeland of my heart.

We met friends there that became family, and we learned to love that country and its people with a deep passion. The beauty and history of Ethiopia are unmatched, and almost ten years after leaving it, I still miss it. This book is my love letter to a place I adored and that adored me right back.

Even though Elias is a fictional character the challenges faced by the LGBTQI+ in Ethiopia are very real. Many have had to seek exile in other countries in order to live and love openly and without fear. The *House of Guramayle* is an organization whose mission is to advocate for the safety and health of the Ethiopian LGBTQI+ community. For more information on how to support their work, visit their website at: https://houseofguramayle.org/

ACKNOWLEDGMENTS

Finding Joy was the first story I sat down to write. I am filled with gratitude that it is now out in the world and for those who helped me in this journey.

To my partner, Andrew, whose wanderlust matches mine perfectly and when we met had already set his eyes on Ethiopia. A place that is such a big part of our love story.

To all the friends and colleagues who in the last few years have read versions of this book and given me such valuable feedback.

To Mackenzie Walton, my editor. You really helped me find ways to make Desta Joy and Elias shine, thank you.

To Leni Kauffman who created the beautiful illustration for this cover. I wanted two brown, queer men embracing in joy, and I wanted the beautiful Ethiopian savanna in the background. That was exactly what I got.

To my writing community, you are such a support and blessing.

And finally to Ethiopia, I cherish the years I called Addis Ababa home. To every person I met in that time who made me feel welcome and like I was exactly where I needed to be.

ABOUT THE AUTHOR

Adriana was born and raised in the Caribbean, but for the last fifteen years has let her job (and her spouse) take her all over the world. She loves writing stories about people who look and sound like her people, getting unapologetic happy endings.

When she's not dreaming up love stories, planning logistically complex vacations with her family or hunting for discount Broadway tickets, she's a trauma therapist in New York City, working with survivors of domestic and sexual violence.

Her Dreamers series, has been featured on Entertainment Weekly, The Washington Post, NPR, and was one of the TODAY Show on NBC's Hot Beach Reads picks. She's one of the co-creators of the Queer Romance PoC Collective. Visit her at: adrianaherreraromance.com

twitter.com/ladrianaherrera
instagram.com/ladriana_herrera

CPSIA information can be obtained
at www.ICGtesting.com
Printed in the USA
LVHW090010170621
690392LV00004B/971